PACIFIC APOCALYPSE

and the

RIVER OCEAN

a screenplay by

P. A. FITZGERALD

Pacific Apocalypse
and the
River Ocean
ISBN 978-0-6456581-1-8
First published 2023

Cover design by
Graham Davidson
Typesetting by Rack and Rune Publishing
https://rackandrune.com

RACK & RUNE
publishing

Foreword

My first response to the gob-smackingly arrogant and senseless sinking of Greenpeace's Rainbow Warrior—by Gallic Spooks in Auckland Harbour in 1985 which also killed a Portuguese environmentalist—was total disbelief; my second response, however, was my 135-page novella *The Journeyman*, written in anger about a fictional group of female and male ecological warriors as they made their way to Muroroa atoll to protest the then subterranean Nuclear Testing by France's Force du Frappe. Just prior to the advent of the World Wide Web, I turned this short novel into *Pacific Meltdown*, my first screenplay, and garnered immediate international creative interest and initial financial backing from some genuine high flyers.

Next, thing I knew, I had an Agent and it had attached a just pre-*Gladiator* co-lead in Russell Crowe, an ensemble cast of name Australian actors and a talented production team. It had also attracted a valuable tabled co-production offer from newly emergent NL company Bergen-Egmond, which was mistakenly rejected, as they were destined to win Best Foreign Film for *Antonia's Line*, two years later before morphing into major company *Eyeworks*.

A group of elite Newcastle businessmen and 3 BRW Rich List development investors then materialized, including a Billionaire W.A Mining magnate. But Time was short and a legal glitch held up the prospectus just after Paul Hogan's third Dundee film failed at the Box Office. Despite the Financial Review's suggesting my film looked the best of the 9 local film investments in the marketplace that year, the prospectus was issued late and the film narrowly went down. I eventually re-discovered my focus and wrote other strong stories before totally rewriting my first geopolitical story as *Pacific Apocalypse & The River Ocean* a wide-ranging mini epic seen through the eyes of a brave Australian farming and soldiering family no great distance from Narrabri and Pillega. Its sub-story parallels the past and growing Pacific climate and nuclear waste dilemmas and shows a glancing history of this ocean and as it traces the fortunes of a community in some of our agricultural heartlands located along semi-fictional Ocean River. It turns a hunting spotlight on the darker doings of some reckless Multi-Nationals and their insatiable search of fossil fuels and precious metals. The story discovers ordinary heroes fighting for protecting the land and water security and it exposes the growing deterioration of former paradises and those who use the ocean, rivers and valuable land as something to be totally exploited, or as a garbage dump, and a place to mine, ruin and over fish. The new story also highlights the aftermath of Muroroa and Fangataufa atmospheric Testing and references the near 100,000 people in French Polynesia now likely eligible for compensation due to exposure to lethal levels of radiation during the earlier atmospheric Tests and as a consequence of other nearby disasters. All these stories are woven into a compelling compressed real and engaging semi fictional human story taking place in these former Edens. But this is no documentary as this story is told in the form of a steadily mounting thriller featuring some very real players.

Industry readers to date have labelled my new story a compelling credible thriller which if read by the right Producer - and or Director from "Anywhere"- will be seriously sourced in order to get it made for the Cinema or for a Streaming Service: without doubt!

P. A. Fitzgerald

PACIFIC APOCALYPSE
&
THE RIVER OCEAN

FIRST DRAFT
By
Peter Anthony Fitzgerald

OPEN ON SATELLITE'S IDYLLIC VIEW OF PACIFIC FROM SPACE: THE VISION SKIMS OVER ISLANDS AND OCEAN

SUPER: SOUTH PACIFIC 1995

#1 INT. LUXURY YACHT "CORSAIR" SOUTH PACIFIC. DAY

O/H POV: A VERDANT PACIFIC ISLAND

A MAN stands on a strip of beach. Beyond is a CORAL REEF, over which, small waves roll. CLOSE: Myriad FISH species and other sea creatures can be seen in the clear lagoon.

Suddenly "THE HAND OF GOD" appears. It picks up the "TINY MAN" and drops him into the lagoon. CCU shows it's actually just a realistic miniature toy.

WIDE shows this to be a magnificent PACIFIC BIOSPHERE and a stunted actual MAN (AUGUSTIN KRANEK,71) is playing GULLIVER, or GOD, with this LILLIPUTIAN CONSTRUCTION. The MINIATURE WORLD looks to-scale and operates as a microcosm of the real thing, thanks to COMPUTERIZED N.A.S.A TECHNOLOGY. The ISLAND even boasts a wonderful Bonsai jungle. Images of the REAL PACIFIC can be seen through viewing windows on one side of the CORSAIR'S opulent Entertainment room. MLS reveal the CORSAIR's a "10 Star LUXURY" MOTORIZED SUPER YACHT. ELSEWHERE in this Entertainment area is a deluxe BAR, as well as a convincing model EUROPEAN RAILWAY system and a displayed scaled-forest, with farms, villages and so on. PAN TO:

In another corner under a billiard table-sized glass case, sits a splendid MINIATURE MIXED EUCALYPT AND RAINFOREST with TREES and plants 10-20 centimetres high. There's also a clearing in the middle of the forest. The Title on the casing reads: JABINGARRA FOREST AUSTRALIA: KRANEK ENTERPRISES. It's easy to get the impression that KRANEK has some kind of Messianic complex. FADE TO BLACK

#2 EXT/INT DREAM SEQUENCE POLYNESIAN WAR CANOE. DAY

FADE IN: THE IMAGE is out of FOCUS. There's an abrupt explosion of deep blue and green and an almighty "VRHOOMFF! VRHOOMFF! VRHOOMFF! sound against the thunder and ROAR of BIG WAVES.

Suddenly a massive WAKA TAUA POLYNESIAN WAR CANOE shoots into FRAME. It crests waves and scuds down the other steep sides and races towards unseen ENEMIES, as 60 massive WARRIOR OARSMAN with fierce facial and body TATTOOS suddenly break into a chilling rhythmical chanting as their massive outrigger canoe ploughs through the daunting OCEAN.

#3 FISHING BOAT DECK. PACIFIC.DAY

CLOSE ON a Formidable SAMOAN MAN regaining consciousness after dreaming of his ANCESTORS rowing to WAR. CUT TO:

#4 EXT. A QANTAS PILOT'S POINT OF VIEW SKIMS OVER THE PACIFIC

From the PILOT'S POV there's a tiny white SPECK on the vast OCEAN. A SLOW ZOOM on the speck reveals a luxury fishing boat.

#5 EXT.PACIFIC AND LUXURY FISHING BOAT.DAY

The SAMOAN MAN, FELITI VAIA (mid-twenties, trussed and bound, has facial-welts, bruises and a swollen black eye)sprawls on the forward DECK near the CABIN.

His eyes finally FOCUS enough to see big GAME FISHING rods and Harness gear. The motor is off and the BOAT bobs in the big swell. FELITI'S memory "visibly" returns. He knows he's in a bad place and watches the 5 EUROPEAN-LOOKING FISHERMEN standing in a bunched group by the Transom near the stern.

#6 EXT.INT. LUXURY FISHING BOAT. SOUTH PACIFIC. MORNING

These MEN look like Military. They argue the fate of their CAPTIVE, but he can't hear them. They're drinking heavily.

> JAPIE(AFRIKAANER ACCENT, IRONIC)
> You're talking bullshit HERVE. 'E's not just a sodding NUISANCE: this particular KAFFIR is a...

He flicks his head at FELITI. CLIVE OPENS A CAN OF BEER

> CLIVE (AUSTRALIAN ACCENT)
> He's a bloody SAMOAN, JAPIE, not a bloody KAFFIR!

> JAPIE
> Fallatio fallartio ! 'E's not just a unifying FIGURE to the KANNAKA people: e's also a gutsy and dangereuse POLYNESIAN DONKIE KONT,

7

> JAPIE (cont)
>
> aren't you FELITI? Notwithstanding, SOLDIERS' etiquette demands 'ee deserves a good, clean death: Such as a bullet to his coconut cranium!

The SOUTH AFRICAN takes a SMITH and WESSON 45 from his belt. FELITI sees this and shuts his eyes for a moment and sees another fleeting image of his ANCESTORS in the WAR CANOE.

> MARC (FRENCH ACCENT)
>
> Exactement! And Little KRAKEN wants him deceased before MONDAY! This one has kill at least three GENDARMES and two CALDOCHES, even if ze JURY could not agree it proved. So if he disappear just like...

He clicks his fingers

> We don't make him MARTYR. I vote for bullet also.

> CLIVE (DRUNKEN AUSSIE ACCENT)
>
> Or..how's about we offer him a secret HERO's death that only him and us'll know about and respect: offer him a beau geste..

The OTHERS look at CLIVE as if he's on Psychedelic drugs a "beau geste":

> ...a last tiny chance of escape before he dies bravely. After all, it's almost twenty five miles of shark-infested ocean to the nearest land! That's a worthy death for such an enemy as him. It's what he would want and what the BASTARD deserves: No question!

He looks around the group one by one and they all nod agreement. MOVING: FELITI's, powerful, and fights hard. It takes ALL of them to drag him to the edge of the STERN. CLIVE cuts FELITI'S leg bindings but not those binding his hands, and they instantly hurl him in. CLIVE drops a SWISS ARMY KNIFE near him, which FELITI dives for and manages to retrieve. He treads water while he cuts the ropes off his hands and swears at his TORMENTORS in SAMOAN.

> CLIVE
> Nice catch-recover. It's SWISS Army issue, and the gift that keeps on giving. It's good for opening boxes of Swiss chocolates, cutting toenails and cutting rope, but for staving off SEA MONSTERS? Not so much! We heard you're a pretty good swimmer FELITI, so I reckon we should expect to see you back in NOUMEA some time... though most likely being cut out of the belly of a five metre MAKO shark.

> HEINZ (LAUGHING, GERMAN ACCENT)
> Yeah, sure we'll be seeing him alright: In the next life.

They all laugh as the ISLANDER treads water swearing at them in the SAMOAN and DREHU languages.

> FELITI
> You fucking DRUMLINE MERCENARIES will go to the Guillotine for what you've done to our people. I swear vengeance on all of you!

> HERVE (ANOTHER FRENCH ACCENT)
> Feisty BASTARD isn't he! Tant pis! We do not speak SAMOAN or DREHU, FELITI, and NO, you CAN'T come back on board and have some prawns and beers. Adieu!

He abruptly pulls out a gun and fires it into the air

> HERVE LE MAITRE
> Ze starter pistol has sound...
> He now tips a bucket of bloody fish entrails into
> the water.

> CLIVE
> Better start free-styling mate. I think I hear
> TIGERS approaching. Try not to piss yourself
> 'cause they say pee attracts them like blood does..

FELITI swims away from the area as fast as he can. When he looks back, several fins start appearing around the fishing boat. He can sees the MEN open more cans of beer and start fishing and laughing. They all glance at him occasionally as he swims at a steady pace towards low cloud hovering over what may be rising-land, in the far distance.

#7 EXT. WIDE. PACIFIC OCEAN AND ISLAND BEACH.DAY

A SERIES OF DISSOLVES from different POVS – from above, from behind and underwater - show FELITI swimming for his life, even through jelly fish that sting his face and body a couple of times. An approaching fin scares him for a moment but it's just a DOLPHIN that swims close to check him out.

He strokes tirelessly and with stony determination. Every now and again he closes his eyes for a few seconds and mentally "sees" his wife and young children outside their village hut and calling soundlessly to him to keep striving to reach them. DISSOLVE TO:

Fatigue finally sets in. He slows and looks ready to pass out. But suddenly he sees a distant glimmer of land, then smiles and finds a second wind. He sometimes ducks his head under water as he swims. With only about a mile to the sliver of beach of a green ISLAND, he stops suddenly and stares ahead numbly, treading water.

About 80 metres in front of him and blocking his path to the ISLAND are five TIGER SHARKS in a half circle almost "as if having a meeting" and two are directly facing him. He closes his eyes for a last vision of his WARRIOR ANCESTORS in the War Canoe and fires up ONE MORE TIME. He now swims directly at them at full pace. And miraculously, when he reaches them, they leisurely move several metres apart and allow him to swim straight through unharmed. As he continues, on he prays aloud.

                    FELITI
        Praise to TAGALOA, GOD of our people

As the sun sinks on the horizon, FELITI drags himself up on the narrow beach and slowly jogs along a jungle path running parallel to the beach. Shortly he arrives at a village with a few boats, some with outboards, lined up near the shoreline.

#8 EXT/INT.P.D EXTERPRISES BUILDING.NOUMEA.EARLY EVENING

This fortress-like FRENCH COLONIAL building looks like a former PRISON. Closed-circuit TV Monitors watch outside and in.

P.D ENTERPRISES ADVENTURE AND ECO TOURISM occupy the bottom floor. There are glossy posters of magic islands, reefs and exotic wildlife. A large flat-screen screen TV in the plate glass window streams loops of Dives to World War 11 Wrecks, coral reefs, jungle getaways and romantic beaches.

There's a tough uniformed Military MAN at a desk in the entrance. He wears a holstered-gun. It's wall-to-wall closed Circuit TVs. Another EUROPEAN MAN in a lightweight suit enters the building, nods to the guard and athletically mounts a staircase.

MOVING: Upstairs the lengthy office also has plate glass windows and stylish wooden Venetian blinds: All closed. Another armed MAN sits in the RECEPTION area outside this office as well. It's very different from the one downstairs.

The black COPPERPLATE writing (in French with English sub titles)on the window reads: P.D ENTERPRISES SECURITY: Special Service Provisions for Companies and Individuals: Inclusive of Security for major Functions and Clubs. A slightly smaller font below it reads: P.D.ENTERPRISES LOAN COLLECTION AGENCY:

Guaranteed successful outcomes FOR ALL Loan Retrieval. The third entry in an even smaller font. It reads PELAGIC DRUMLINE ENTERPRISES : DIRECT ACTION. The accompanying small dark print requires close inspection, but reads:

INFORMATION GATHERING; PRIVATE DETECTION CONTRACTS; MULTI LEVEL PROBLEM SOLUTIONS; INTELLIGENCE GATHERING INITIATIVES; SEARCH AND RETRIEVAL; PROOF OF LIFE; LEDGER ADJUSTMENT; PEST CONTROL; EQUALIZATION;REDRESSING IMBALANCES. ALL WORTHY CAUSES CONSIDERED.

#9 EXT.INT.RUN DOWN HOUSE IN KANNAK AREA.

MORNING   FELITI's family are hurriedly packing up all of their things with ELOI, a family friend. FELITI sits in a car hidden among trees, its engine running. They take what they can carry and FELITI drives off down back-roads.

#9B EXT PELAGIC DRUMLINE OFFICES. NEW CALEDONIA. NIGHT

FELITI is unrecognizable in a black tracksuit and beanie, as he scales the back wall of PELAGIC DRUMLINE with grappling hooks and ropes. A drugged Doberman guard dog sleeps directly below him with a half-eaten baited meat pie. From a ledge near the top of the building FELITI lobs two MOLOTOV COCKTAILS through the narrow windows and they let off loud explosions and start instant fires. There's yelling and cursing from inside the building and soon fire engines can be heard, but FELITII's already 100 metres away and running hard. He's picked up by a black car that appears as if from nowhere and disappears into the night. DISSOLVE TO:

#10 EXT.REMOTE SOUTHERN NEW CALEDONIAN ISLAND. MORNING

FELITI, his wife and two young sons arrive at a remote island in a speed boat and transfer with their suitcases to an old sloop with a crew of fellow ISLANDERS.

> FELITI(IN DREHU WITH SUBTITLES)
> Many thanks old friend. I owe you..
> ELOI (HANDING HIM MONEY)
> Nothing! You can get to North Queensland with this AUSTRALIAN currency and work permit and stay with some of our relatives. Get labouring work and fruit picking…but keep your head down. You are a hero for what you did. God be with you and your family.

#11 INT.OCEAN RIVER HOTEL. WAYNTON N.S.W DUSK 1995

It's the end of the working day and the OCEAN RIVER HOTEL is filling up. It's a typical country PUB with people selling meat tray raffles, playing Pool, drinking and yarning. Someone turns off the booming JUKE BOX for a BREAKING NEWS BROADCAST on a BIG SCREEN TELEVISION.

Growing numbers watch as FRENCH PRESIDENT JACQUES CHIRAC appears (with sub titles) stating the FRENCH GOVERNMENT intends recommencing NUCLEAR TESTING in "cette anee (this year) 1995" and the following year,1996,at MORUROA and FANGATAUFA atolls in the TUOMOTU islands. Some insults are hurled at the TV.

Next, Dutch Ecologist WIM JARED appears in response. He is shown in a CORNER SQUARE of the TV SCREEN, as the main screen area features documentary FOOTAGE accompanying his words: The FOOTAGE shows earlier Pacific nuclear TESTS, PROTEST confrontations, RAINBOW WARRIOR's sinking and SCIENTISTS' dire warnings.

> WIM JARED (30)
> I listened in utter disbelief to French PRESIDENT JACQUES CHIRAC's appalling decision to resume NUCLEAR TESTING at the two atolls. Vast areas of the South Pacific marine environment have already been catastrophically damaged. In 1977 an atmospheric Test showered TAHITI with 500 times more than the maximum allowable level of PLUTONIUM. Everyone everywhere should be alarmed by the fact 85% of all VETERANS and WORKERS exposed to the MORUROA Test site have MYELOID LEUKEMIA and THYROID CANCERS. THAT'S 85% percent!!

On the other side of the room a couple of teenage Youths start the Juke box and a scuffle breaks Out with another group who want to listen to the TV. The brief fight drowns out the TV speech.

> WIM JARED (CONT)
> Sophisticated Computer technology can now simulate these weapon Tests and their results, yet CHIRAC's determined to ignore World

WIM JARED (CONT)

opinion and physically Test Neutron bombs near vulnerable populated areas. It now needs restating that in a 1979 Test, the Nuclear device remained stuck half way down the 800 metre deep chamber and, incredibly, the decision was made to detonate anyway. While it caused only an initial small tidal wave and some nuclear effluent leakage, it in fact caused a major 2 kilometre long fracture in the atoll that was metres wide in places. Some of the atoll surface is now actually underwater, which means part of the island has broken off.

WIM JARED

Some respected VOLCANOLOGISTS claim it inevitable, even without another detonation, something catastrophic, will occur. Our organization, SENTINEL, will joining a Greenpeace flotilla of PROTEST VESSELS to end this disgusting irresponsible decision. FRANCE is also currently beset by conflict with FLNKS, the INDIGENOUS KANAK INDEPENDENCE MOVEMENT in NEW CALEDONIA, now fighting for their independence, which is another black eye for them. In no way do we have any issue with FRANCE's wishes for a EUROPEAN Nuclear deterrent against the growing SOVIET nuclear arsenals but this smug superior attitude harks back to BRITAIN and the U.S's similarly arrogant Testing in the PACIFIC and AUSTRALIA in the 1950's. EUROPEANS and AMERICANS won't stand for Testing in their own countries and from now on neither will Pacific Nations! Not in our back yard, Monsieur CHIRAC! We demand a NUCLEAR FREE PACIFIC.

The final confronting moving images show AUSTRALIAN SURFER IAN COHEN hanging onto the prow of a Nuclear Armed AMERICAN destroyer sailing into SYDNEY HARBOUR.

It's a brave but incredibly dangerous surfing stunt and a compelling IMAGE about what's at stake, and the dangers of NUCLEAR. Most WAYNTON LOCALS are on-side with WIM'S sentiments and some clap, whistle or cheer the lone SURFER.

#12 INT.OCEAN RIVER HOTEL. DAY

At one table a solid Polynesian man in a WAYNTON GOANNAS football jumper watches the screen with a couple of AUSTRALIAN MATES.

> VUNI
> Right on BROTHER! What he said! Give it to those arrogant BASTARDS. That nuclear shit stuffed the fish even way across in Raratonga …

#13 EXT QUEENSLAND. ROAD THROUGH RAINFOREST CITY-FRINGE DUSK.

Two solidly built males - WIM JARED and NED BAKER (28) - are running down a steep and deserted road shortly before SUNDOWN. The road bisects RAINFOREST with occasional five metre drops either side. They're setting a good pace and their conversation is laconic as CICADAS shrilling from the bush make it hard to hear. DISSOLVE

The RUNNERS surprise 3 ROSELLAS on the road. The MEN turn their jolting heads to watch them fly away screeching.

PAN TO: Further back up the road behind them an old black UTILITY TRUCK without number plates, rolls onto the road from a concealed dirt track and its headlights come on. The DRIVER clutch-starts it, revs loudly and speeds up.

The TOWN below transitions into a twinkling FAIRYLAND as the sun begins to slip below the horizon and street and house lights come on. NED BAKER stretches out now and his friend also runs faster.

Suddenly high beam car-lights discover them on a part of

the road with steeper falls to jungle either side. WIM's shocked and calls out a warning as he jumps towards a roadside tree.

> WIM
> Watch out! Jump NED..!

NED turns his head just in time to see WIM leaping off the road. NED leaps high too, but glances off the UTE's bonnet and flies over the edge of the drop into a copse of tall ferns just before the ledge drops away more steeply again. DISSOLVE

#14 INT/EXT GOLD COAST CAVILL AVE BEACH FRONT HOTEL 1995.DAY

NED BAKER and his younger BROTHER WILL (26) are having a beer in a beachfront BAR. NED'S snappily dressed. WILL wears Australian ARMY fatigues. WILL's brought some old family photos he passes over to his brother.

> WILL
> So, yesterday's excitement makes it about the seventh.. or is it the eighth of your nine lives you've now used up? What did the COPS say?

NED (IRONIC)

Yeah you're correct, WILL, we're NOT dead, but we sure as hell could have been! Cops said heaps of DRIVERS wouldn't have seen us and a few would have done a bolt, just as that driver did…but

WILL (SHAKING HIS HEAD)

Course I get how you must feel, but it would have been bloody hard to see you.

NED (KNOCKS HIS KNUCKLES ON WILL'S HEAD)

Hello! Anyone home? Two days ago WIM's on national TV News as the main ORGANIZER of a Nuclear protest flotilla to MORUROA and last night he and his lawyer are almost killed a by a hit-run driver? Join the dots DOPEY.

WILL

You're not seriously suggesting the DRIVER targeted you both? Was the guy wearing a beret, smoking Gauloise and driving a CITROEN or some-such?

NED

Take the piss all you like, but you weren't there! Anyway, that kind of thing goes on all over the world all the time now. There's high unemployment in South America and Eastern Europe and plenty of well- trained professional SOLDIERS looking for paid work. Anywhere!
So yeah, we were deliberately targeted! I know it. Anyway…it's good you're joining the Australian ARMY though. They'll make a man of you.

WILL

In that case maybe you ought to join before I do NANCY!

NED thumps him on the arm.

> NED
>
> But I don't like your odds of getting into the S.A.S. They're very selective.

> WILL
>
> Yeah, well the two S.A.S COLONELS who interviewed me said my results were good, and they liked my chances.

> NED
>
> Great! So, BRO, with me sailing the blue PACIFIC and you heading for PERTH, we mightn't catch up for a while.

> WILL
>
> One thing I still don't get though is how come corporate Money Bags Lawyer NED BAKER is actually working for the

> WILL
>
> Environment without charging a thousand bucks an hour for it. That's a GODDAM MIRACLE is what it is!

He suddenly pauses and looks NED in the eye as if calculating something. And then a light switch goes on.

> WILLIAM
>
> Ha...aang on! Wait up! I thought I your shnoz was growing! The actual real reason you're going wouldn't happen to be because you've met SOMEONE.

He closes his eyes and touches his temples with his index fingers like a HOLLYWOOD PSYCHIC.

> WILL
> I'm seeing... a strawberry Blonde
> ENVIRONMENTALIST. About yeah high
> He raises the flat of his hand to five foot 5 And
> with magnificent titties; maybe models lingerie
> and swimwear for a magazine. Am I getting close?

> NED
> JOANNA's an A Grade JOURNALIST
> SMART-ARSE! And she'll be here in five minutes,
> so don't embarrass me.

WILL chuckles to himself and then shows NED a few old PHOTOS of when they were about 12 and 14 and sitting on horses outside their 19TH century HOMESTEAD. There's a high windbreak in deep background plus a LONE PINE TREE at a distance. Their MOTHER's feeding carrots to the HORSES. The other photo shows a majestic property. The sign above the entrance gate reads LONE PINE HISTORIC FARM AND HOMESTEAD 1846. It's beautiful country and obviously prime farming land.

> NED BAKER
> So I guess it'll be 12 years or more before you retire
> as a MAJOR or something with a full Pension.
> Either that or a free FUNERAL and all the
> trimmings: Which-ever comes first. Don't forget
> MUM and DAD will need your help at LONE
> PINE for a couple of years when you get out of
> the ARMY. They'll be too old to manage. When
> the inevitable happens, we'll get a great price for
> that land. Some very big companies are already
> hovering around certain farming properties in
> RAINFOREST VALLEY from what I hear.

WILL suddenly looks shocked.

WILL

What the hell are you talking about selling LONE PINE? That property's been in our family 150 years!

I'll be the one managing it after the ARMY and I sure as hell won't be selling it to any fucking CARPET-BAGGERS from anywhere overseas or any ROBBER BARON MINING companies. I'll pay YOU out, brother.

They look at each other in mutual stunned silence.

NED

Jesus! You're serious! It never once crossed my mind you'd ever consider a farmer's life! Anyway, you couldn't afford to buy me out given what it's worth ...MINING means progress for this country WILL

WILL

It's common knowledge COAL MINING is a dead end industry with no future and its stuffs up farming lands, the atmosphere and the rivers. The Animal metaphor equivalent to what COAL MINING does, is the WOMBAT, cos basically speaking, "the wombat eats, roots and leaves."

Are you sure we're really BROTHERS? I can't believe you'd even contemplate selling it. We lived most of our lives on THAT property; in THAT Valley. That homestead and that land is in your and my DNA!

NED (PRETENDS TO PLAY A TINY VIOLIN)

Of course I've got some great memories of the place. But boys grow up and move on while parents get old and pass on. You're not the marrying and family type, So why would you want the hassle of LONE PINE. It will make us rich.

WILL

You're already rich you dumb bastard! It's where I want to live when the ARMY's done with me. Eventually I want to be buried here.

NED

I could arrange that this arvo!

WILL BAKER

I mean it. I won't allow you to sell it! Not under any circumstance!

NED

WON'T allow? You WON'T have a bloody choice. MUM and DAD's WILL states we are to be joint INHERITORS. There's a couple of things I really DO know, and that's FAMILY LAW and CONTRACT LAW.

WILLIAM

They'd change that bloody Will if they heard what you just said and if you persist with this I swear I'll tell them your intentions.

NED'S LOOK SAYS WILL WOULD'T DARE

WILL

Watch this space Dipshit!

WILL packs up his haversack and finishes his beer just as an attractive smart looking WOMAN in her mid-twenties approaches the table. NED gets up and kisses her and gets a seat for her.

NED (BOTH BROTHERS ARE FURIOUS)

JOANNA DANIELS, this is my brother WILL and he's..

WILL

Just leaving! Sorry JOANNA. It's nice to meet you. As for you, whatever your name is, I'd like to know just what you did with my brother.

NED gestures with his face and hands in exasperation

WILL

Goodbye NED. Take care of yourself and don't take any undue risks wherever you're going. JOANNA...

He nods to her and starts walking away but JOANNA comes after him and they talk inaudibly. WILL changes his mind and goes to the bar and returns with two beers and a glass of wine.

NED

Forget that other stuff. This might be the last time we see each other for a while. Stay for a drink and a meal. Get to know JOANNA. Will...?

WILL

She's very persuasive your JOURNALIST friend. Not to mention a bona fide stunner.

JOANNA's unimpressed by his well-meaning flattery.

WILL

But you need to remind THIS GUY about Humanity and exactly what Ethics are.

JOANNA grins and NED punches him in the arm again, though the issue's unresolved.

#16 EXT.WAYNTON RURAL COMMUNITY N.S.W. DAY 1995

It's a midweek day in WAYNTON and the growing prosperous town's busy with shoppers, some European and South American backpackers, local farmers buying supplies, and business people coming and going from the Chamber of Commerce, and so on.

MOVING. FROM THE POV of a LOCAL COP walking MAIN STREET. The COP waves to many on his beat. It's hard to imagine he sees much action in this sleepy place. An well-groomed and athletic ABORIGINAL MAN stops to talk to him.

> RUSSELL NAMIDGEE (CHEERFUL WISEGUY)
> G'day WAYNE. I have to say you had an uncharacteristically good footy game at PROP on the weekend MATE. Did'ya manage ter get hold of some of the gear LANCE ARMSTRONG was on?

> WAYNE THE COP
> No, RUSSELL: Gorilla steroids aren't freely available in our town at the moment. What are you up to? Is the Pub closed for renovations?

> RUSSELL (LAUGHING)
> Racial profiling's actually illegal in this country nowadays, BIGFOOT. Actually I was wondering about those OUTSIDERS in black AUDIS been coming through town in the past week. Fat cat ASIAN BLOKES and chubby white fellas in shiny suits. I even saw two shady CANBERRA POLITICIANS with 'em I recognized from the TV. The MAYOR was riding around with one lot looking like he'd just won the Lottery. Twice!

The COP is genuinely surprised.

WAYNE THE COP
Dunno know anything about that! You might be surprised, but the MAYOR doesn't consult with me on Town Business matters.

RUSSELL
That could be 'cause you were banging his ex MISSUS for a while!

WAYNE
That's actually a plausible observation, dickhead. Maybe you could write down those VISITORS' Number-plates if you see them around again as I could easily do a check

SUPER: SOUTH PACIFIC 1995

#16 EXT.INT. SENTINEL KETCH BIG SKY ON THE OPEN SEA.

SUPER: VARIOUS PACIFIC ISLANDS. SUPER:JULY 1995

A SERIES OF DISSOLVES. NED, JOANNA, TORBEN the Danish Captain, Dutch First Mate HANK, CANADIAN Photographer and deckhand JACKSON DREWE (30), AMERICAN SCIENTISTS SUZANNE and AL SCANLON (30),and MARIANIQUE FOCH (late 20's),a FRENCH BELGIAN SEISMOLOGIST who comprise the BIG SKY crew are sailing around various islands and testing the waters and the marine life. DISSOLVE TO:

#17 EXT.TUAVALU PACIFIC ISLAND.

MARIONIQUE and the AMERICAN COUPLE study the rising waters and disappearing MARINE LIFE on the slow-drowning island

#18 EXT.NEW CALEDONIA FRENCH POLYNESIA.DAY

BIG SKY sails into the PORT at NOUMEA where there's a few boats arriving for the flotilla to sail to MUROROA.

#19 EXT.NOUMEA MARINA.DAY

JOANNA interviews some LOCAL FRENCH, GERMAN and KANAK ISLANDERS around the island. JACKSON has his camera and takes a few photos. NED seems apprehensive as many refuse to speak to JOANNA. Others are very hostile. DISSOLVE TO:

#20 EXT. NOUMEA STREET.EARLY NIGHT

NED is walking with JOANNA when they're approached by three tough CAUCASIANS in a side street. They are the AUSTRALIAN MERCENARY CLIVE, as well as HERVE, and HEINZ and their cronies from the fishing boat at the start of the story.

> HERVE
> We see you two doing interviews with PEOPLE. Salop! Hippie merde! You are not welcome here..

> CLIVE (QUIETLY MENACING VOICE)
> I would've thought my fellow AUSSIES would be smarter than to go mindlessly sailing off into wild Oceans like this one. There are dangerous places beyond count out there, if you get my drift. VERY FUCKING DANGEROUS! Mind how you go now, won't you. !

They suddenly depart and disappear into the main street.

> NED
> Meet me at CAFE MONTMARTRE on the main street in an hour. I'm going to follow those SPIVS and get a picture.

#21 EXT. CITY STREETS AND MARINA.

A SERIES OF DISSOLVES. NED follows them at a distance. They board an old grey 30 metre MINESWEEPER with the name MEPHISTO written on the side in small lettering in dark peeling paint. Further along is another name. While it's almost painted out, the letters have several gaps but KR..EK can just be discerned by a sharp eye. NED takes a photo and heads back for JOANNA.

#22 EXT.BIG SKY IN THE SOUTH PACIFIC. 1995

The CREW attend to all the various sailing tasks. NED occasionally films and records

#23 INT.JUNGLE BAR.MALAYSIA NIGHT. 1995

In a TOPLESS BAR in SELINGOR, three of WILL'S S.A.S MATES are barely recognizable in jeans and tee shirts. They're drinking with some Bar Girls but also watching a distressed looking WILL talking into a public phone in a quiet area of the Bar. He's holding a STRAITS TIMES newspaper. PAN TO:

A CLOSE UP of a headline shouts "SENTINEL Ketch BIG SKY Missing in South Pacific: CREW FEARED DEAD." It lists the crew including NED and says the boat was last seen near NOUMEA and believed to be heading for the NUCLEAR TEST ZONE.

> WILL
> Hello? Hello?JOANNA? I've just heard the shocking news? What the Hell's happened. Is there still any hope..?

#24 INT.SPLIT-SCREEN: JOANNA'S HOME & MALAYSIAN BAR. NIGHT

JOANNA'S struggling, tearful and obviously pregnant.

>JOANNA
>
>This is a nightmare that never ends. How could such a thing happen, WILL? We were sailing for three months' mostly researching coral reefs till I got SALMONELLA and had to stay in NOUMEA. I'd been doing a big story on the Independence struggle going on there. We were hated in some quarters and actually got threatened by 3 thugs. One was a pig AUSSIE. It was two nights before Big Sky sailed out. I can't help feeling they could be linked to the disappearance. CUT TO

>WILL (FIGHTING FURY)
>
>Write down every single thing you remember about them. Get SENTINEL to pay an artist to do mock ups of them.

>JOANNA (BADLY SHAKEN)
>
>TORBEN, the Big Sky Captain discussed going to MORUROA before the protest flotilla did. There was no further communication after that via radio or phone! You know, BIG SKY was a very sturdy vessel WILL and the CAPTAIN and FIRST MATE were world class SAILORS. It's too sea-worthy to just sink. And NED...

HER VOICE STARTS SHAKING NOW

>WILL
>
>I hear you. Hope for the best, but somehow you have to be prepared for the worst. Always! I have to tell you I won't be attending any counterfeit funeral for him either - not until we know exactly what happened. Call me if I can ever do anything to help. I'll be thinking of you and praying for you as well as NED.

JOANNA
There's something else too, WILL: I'm pregnant
with NED's DAUGHTER. He wanted to call her
VICTORIA

WILL's choked up and can only whisper.

WILLIAM
Well..that's wonderful JOANNA - one great thing!
And it gives me genuine HOPE. Goodbye for now.

WILL returns proceeds to get drunk with the OTHERS.

SUPER: PRESENT DAY BRISBANE AUSTRALIA

#26 EXT. BRISBANE HEADQUARTERS ALL POINTS GLOBAL

The SIGN on the OFFICE door reads: ALL POINTS GLOBAL:
VICTORIA DANIELS-BAKER. LEGAL EXECUTIVE.

VICKY's now 23 and all grown up. She's a stylish and savvy high
flying LAWYER for this huge company. ALL POINTS GLOBAL are
all about money and power and VICKY seems to fit that mould
exactly. On her luxury cedar desk there's a photo of JOANNA
with VICKY as a little GIRL and a photo of NED BAKER, his
BROTHER WILL and JOANNA' taken at the PUB before NED left
AUSTRALIA forever. PAN TO:

A nervous young MAN of about 18 wearing an ill-fitting suit knocks
and enters her office.

TRAVIS
Excuse me MS DANIELS-BAKER, I'm your new
INTERN, TRAVIS SMITH, reporting for work.
They told me to introduce myself and you'd tell
me my tasks.

> VICKY (SHE'S VERY FORMAL)
> Hello TRAVIS. Ask my P.A RENAE for the hard copies of the KRANEK SEED GENETICS COPYRIGHT and one of the AUSTRALIAN GRAIN SEED PATENTS USBs

> TRAVIS
> Yes MS DANIELS-BAKER.
> He's about to close the door after him

> VICKY
> Oh, and you might want to see about getting a new suit if you're to be here for a few months. Maybe RALPH LAUREN..

TRAVIS looks humiliated and is obviously cash-strapped. Like her father VICKY seems short on empathy.

#27 INT.CORSAIR LUXURY-CRUISER TECH-HUB ROOM. PACIFIC OCEAN. DAY

CCU OF KRANEK'S BONSAI JABINGARRA RAINFOREST FOREST COMES INTOFOCUS. Suddenly KRANEK'S chubby fingers place a YELLOW DUMP TRUCK IN A CLEARING in this mini FOREST. ECU ON THE MARKINGS ON THE TRUCK READ BIO-KRANEK GLOBAL.

KRANEK'S a short, slightly portly MAN with a patina of Hollywood flash. He seems almost hermetically sealed in this floating palace. He's dressed in a CLEVELAND CAVALIERS TEE SHIRT COVERED BY AN EXPENSIVE CASUAL SUIT, AND WEARS MOCCASINS without socks. TORSTEN, one of his senior offsiders, a tough Scandinavian in Military fatigues, enters the area.

KRANEK (SHOUTING UNNECESSARILY)
SOMEONE Bring me the SEISMIC projections for the COOK ISLANDS and VILA. When the MORUROA HD DIGITAL IMAGINING we did for the FROGS comes through I want to know immediately. And get me that VULCANOLOGIST in here when you do; or on SKYPE at least. What's his name?

TORSTEN
VINCENT PETERS - Doctor VINCENT PETERS

KRANEK
Right! I want to see him the instant those data readings are ready for initial assessment.
He yells for a WAITER and one arrives within seconds

KRANEK
Get me a tall glass of PISCO, will you, MORGAN. The sun's already over the yardarm.

MORGAN(MUTTERS TO SELF AS HE WALKS AWAY)
I wish you were over the bloody yardarm!

#28 INT. BAR AREA KRANEK PACIFIC SHIP. DAY

The white uniformed WAITER continues into the BAR area and speaks to the attractive THAI BARMAID.

MORGAN THE WAITER
Hi LIN. Get me a large glass of PISCO for LITTLE KRAKEN would you?

She looks at him blankly

PIK
I Sorry, only here one week and my ENGLISH good not yet. Who is LITTLE KRAKEN and what is PISCO.

MORGAN (PICKS UP A PAD AND PENCIL)
PISCO is that white PERUVIAN alcoholic drink on the top shelf up there. And a KRAKEN was an ancient and terrible sea monster like maybe a giant squid - with horrible tentacles going everywhere.

He does a quick fair sketch of one grabbing a HUMAN.

MORGAN
And the Name of our short and scary BOSS is AUGUSTIN KRANEK

She's still confused. He writes the letters K R A N E K out and changes the letter order to show her the anagram.

LIN (FINALLY NODDING)
Ahhhh!

#29 INT. MAIN LOUNGE AREA KRANEK SUPER YACHT.DAY

MOVING: KRANEK walks around in his S.O.T.A TECH CENTRE speaking to nerdy MEN and WOMEN seated at SUPER COMPUTERS. They simultaneously watch a substantial CENTRALLY PLACED INTERACTIVE SCREEN with moving data and SCATTERGUN GRAB IMAGES OF VARIOUS WORLD LOCATIONS OF KRANEK developments. PAN TO:

TORSTEN
AUGUSTIN, you'll want to know the good news from our BAYONVILLE Team on the new TRICERATOPS STEALTH VEHICLE prototypes. NATO have given Fourth Tier approval for an initial run of two thousand, contingent upon final testing by the chief structural and mechanical engineers in FRANKFURT and DUSSELDORF. And the STEALTH DIRT BIKE prototype is also good to go!

KRANEK
Great news TORSTEN! And what of the CSG DRILL? How diluted is the noise factor now.

TORSTEN
The first two models are fully operational and can be shipped to AUSTRALIA in a matter of weeks.

KRANEK is elated at this news.

KRANEK
Now you're cooking with gas!
Just watch our stocks move on WALL STREET, the FTSIE and HANG SEN when this info is made public.
And lastly, for now, how's the RAINFOREST VALLEY acquisition for MINING leases progressing? And what of THE FOREST itself?

TORSTEN shrugs negatively. KRANEK's quick to anger.

TORSTEN
This will be no easy matter. The FARMERS and Ag communities are more organized now and even some of the Radio SHOCK JOCKS are against us on this one...

KRANEK'S mood grows darker.
Of course many of their POLITICIANS are in our pockets. Their greed makes them useful. But the ordinary AUSTRALIANS are starting to wake up – they're getting more politically active and organizing demonstrations and boycotts against our Group.

KRANEK
I have a very limited time frame for OCEAN RIVER and the JABINGARRA FOREST. And no wild bunch of Hick Pricks are going to hold up this great Southern Enterprise. That land is the future EL DORADO of the SOUTHERN HEMISPHERE. All Testing to date verifies A CORNUCOPIA of RESOURCES - GOLD, SILVER, URANIUM - and that FOREST is DIAMONDS: I can feel it! It may be time for our friends from PELAGIC DRUMLINE to do what they do best.

TORSTEN knows THIS LOT and is suddenly concerned

TORSTEN
Those PSYCHOPATHS have far too much testosterone and far too much free time on their hands.. not to mention too easy access to lethal weapons! We have to be very careful about sending those MERCENARIES into a developed and democratic country like AUSTRALIA, MISTER KRANEK.

KRANEK
Now there I disagree with you. AUSTRALIA calls itself the LUCKY COUNTRY, not the SMART COUNTRY: many of them even glorify their CONVICT ANCESTORS. Those dopes even let

KRANEK (CONT)

some "reformed" convicts into their first POLICE FORCES and wonder why there was systematic and entrenched Police corruption at a time when RECIDIVISM was sky high. I predict one of their great coming architectural projects will be the biggest prison in the southern hemisphere. They've even got a forger's face on their ten dollar bill for Christ's sake. Ha! Ha! Some Australian CROOKS are smart enough to go into POLITICS too. Up till now their POLITICIANS only seemed to know how to sell off THE LAND or DIG it up. They have not deserved to have a country of such PROMISE until...

Until recently I thought, when they start running short on RESOURCES those Fuckers will be TOTALLY SCREWED..but their new Prime Minister worries me because he wasn't born into money, like the last one.. I think we need to sort this sale before he sorts that country

MOVING. KRANEK moves around interfering randomly with his MICRO WORLDS. An OBSERVER might easily imagine this "GULLIVER" does whatever he wants and takes no prisoners.

ON a mantle-piece he's even assembled a couple of dozen life-like MINIATURE PEOPLE corralled in a glass case with the word STAFF printed on the side. Each "STAFF MEMBER" is on a small stand with his or her name. They're in areas assigned to Ship CREW, Helicopter Pilot, SENIOR EXECUTIVES, MEDIA LEGAL, and SECURITY PELAGIC DRUMLINE but these ones are faceless and unnamed

#30 INT.JAMES COOK UNIVERSITY LECTURE ROOM. PRESENT DAY

A Public lecture's about to commence in a UNI LECTURE THEATRE. The LECTURER(30)looks like a fit and wealthy HIPPIE.

The large Audience comprise a very wide cross section of the PUBLIC and even includes some POLITICIANS and POLICE. Late arrivals look for seats. A TV crew sets up near the front.

The LECTURER recognizes three CORPORATE TYPES entering the Lecture THEATRE. These MEN are dressed casually, but can't hide their arrogance. They're accompanied by a MINDER built like a silverback gorilla "disguised" in an expensive suit.

> BENGT SORENSEN
>
> Good evening. Thank you all for coming. I am BENGT SORENSEN, MARINE BIOLOGIST and RESEARCHER at the SENTINEL CENTRE FOR PACIFIC STUDY AND MANAGEMENT. Our FILM is titled PACIFIC APOCALYPSE and let me tell you that title is no exaggerated hype to get bums on seats: There is irrefutable evidence in our documentary the calamities endured by the PACIFIC Ocean and its human communities in the past seventy years have reached critical mass. We contend that these have now established an irreversible environmental meltdown scenario for the near future.

A few cynical groans are audible among the many gasps. JOANNA DANIELS (49) is among the last arrivals. She's with a distinguished older man. They wave to VICTORIA, who's saved seats for them near the front.

SENTINEL DOCUMENTARY FILM

A SERIES OF DISSOLVES TO THE BYRDS SONG TURN, TURN,

TURN accompanies a nuclear image montage of HIROSHIMOA, NAGASAKI, followed by snatches of DR STRANGELOVE WITH THE CRAZY AMERICAN RIDING THE NUCLEAR BOMB OUT OF THE BOMB BAY, AND THE MONTAGE ENDS WITH THE LAST TIDAL WAVES AND IMAGES OF FUKISHIMA

FILM TITLE: AMERICAN, ENGLISH & FRENCH NUCLEAR TESTS 1954-84

A MELANGE of Black and white footage of atmospheric Tests in the AMERICAN Marshall Islands, English Tests at MONTE BELLO ISLANDS and MARALINGA shows SOLDIERS without protective-gear sweeping down the fallout from plane wings and then THE atmospheric Tests in MORUROA are seen.

The MUSIC heard NOW is a catchy little FRENCH song called AINSI SOIT IL by LOUIS CHEDIDE and it's an ironic MUSICAL accompaniment to the disturbing detonations.

Images of GREENPEACE and then the sinking RAINBOW WARRIOR follow and headlines of the capture of the FRENCH SPIES Alan Mafart & Co who sank it. The Marseillaise plays at discordant speed as do GOD SAVE THE QUEEN and the Star Spangled Banner when theMARALINGA TESTS and BIKINI AND MARSHALL ISLANDS TESTS are seen. The next images in the film are highly confronting.

DOCUMENTARY TITLE: RONGERIK ATOLL MARSHALL ISLANDS 1954.

Half a dozen young POLYNESIAN KIDS are seen playing Softball on a beautiful Pacific island's beach.

Two kids run to catch a fly ball.

The image SLOWLY DISSOLVES into crackly old B&W footage.

An AMERICAN narrates the documentary. At first glance it seems to be a very similar setting to the beginning images, but in fact, it's a chilling dark-mirror version. The scratchy film becomes alarming when we we're told the CHILDREN are playing in the nuclear fall-out because they think it's snow.

#30B INT/EXT COURTHOUSE THE HAGUE.PRESENT

An angry elderly man in traditional FIJIAN attire holds up a newspaper with headlines stating the numbers of ISLANDS in danger of sinking under rising seas.

> RATU SEMU
> The proof is conclusive. The great colonial powers that pillaged the Pacific peoples for hundreds of years must be held responsible and must help us combat the consequences of their reckless actions that have helped cause the heating of the polar ice cap. The only legacy they have left us are catastrophic health and economic problems, through dumping contaminated waste and Nuclear Testing.

#31 NOUMEA.RURAL CEMETERY RURAL JUNGLE SETTING. PRESENT DAY

Two uniformed FRENCH FOREIGN LEGION VETERANS, JEAN LUC (63) and CLAUDE (62) salute a coffin being lowered into a grave and they sing the Marseillaise unaccompanied. There's also an important and formidable looking man of about 40 in a cream suit there. He seems to be there in an official capacity. There are also a couple of young uniformed soldiers and two middle aged

KANAK WOMEN MOURNERS who throw bright flowers on the coffin before the dirt is shovelled in.

> JEAN LUC (IN FRENCH WITH SUBTITLES)
> We are gathered here today to honour and bury our great old friend and comrade GEORGE BLANC.

> CLAUDE (HE IS QUITE ILL LOOKING MAN)
> JEAN LUC and I served with GEORGE in the FOREIGN LEGION in Chad, Dahomey and Serbia and finally on the deadly atoll of MORUROA with the Force Du Frappe.. The Nuclear Defence Arm. And that was where GEORGE contracted the MUROROA LEUKEMIA as they called it. That is what killed GEORGE and not any human enemy. I too contracted that insidious cancer in that terrible place. And soon enough I will be worm meat and having a similar farewell, though with far fewer MOURNERS.

He laughs bitterly. The MAN in the cream suit suddenly stares daggers at CLAUDE and then at JEAN LUC. His articulate look says CLAUDE needs to stop talking immediately.

> JEAN LUC
> What CLAUDE meant to say was that we served with GEORGE in many places. GEORGE was a fine brave soldier and a good man and we will all miss him very much.

#32 INT.NSW STATE SUPREME COURT. DAY

> VICTORIA DANIELS-BAKER
> On behalf of my client C.I.Q Metals, a subsidiary of ALL POINTS GLOBAL,

VICTORIA

your worship, I can categorically and irrefutably state the five readings taken were found to be consistently within the parameters of Department of Health guidelines and never rose above a toxicity of 4.3. Readings were taken from Smokestack three and four and were verified the very same day, in full compliance of all statutes. I therefore submit that Messrs NOAKES and JARDINE, Journalists for the Sentinel Group, and ADAMS NEWSMEDIA, have made a clearly libellous charge against my client, to the effect that there was a sustained emission of noxious gas - the name of which your worship I shall not venture to pronounce at this early hour without my elecution-instructor on hand - but its full chemical name is on the documentation before you

A BUSINESSMEN (65) seated at back studies her with interest. Two JOURNALISTS sitting opposite her look uncomfortable

VICKY

This Government certification then,
She holds up an official looking document unequivocally verifies that it is not the gas named in the charges. I submit that C.I.Q has no case to answer and that Libel is proven.
It's my recommendation that Sentinel publish a comprehensive retraction and apology in all their digital Media and also that they pay damages commensurate with precedent cases such as AMALGAMATED CARBIDE versus BOPAL city.

VICKY packs her papers into her briefcase and leaves. The two JOURNALISTS look at her as if she's pure evil as she heads for the exit, but she manages a wry smile at them. The MAN watching her approaches.

> RUPERT WESTERMAN
>
> Hello VICTORIA. I'm RUPERT WESTERMAN, chief LEGAL EXEC for BIO KRANEK GLOBAL. I wanted to congratulate you on your performance. I've come to tell you BIOKRANEK and ALL POINTS GLOBAL are about to formalize our periodic partnerships and merge as one super company. Despite your youth I see you as having a meteoric future with that company if you're interested.
>
> Thank you Rupert.. I can't deny my ambition and am definitely interested in advancement whatever that might be. I'm not au fait with all of BIOKRANEK's history and long term goals but I shall start researching it immediately.

#33 INT. BRISBANE OFFICES ALL POINTS GLOBAL RESOURCES

The room is a quality fit out. Four middle-aged male Executive "Suits" and one female equivalent, sit around a magnificent long Ash-wood table as VICKY enters. The room features multiple high-tech Media devices, some expensive Australian landscape-Art works, a "prepped" 35 mill projector, photos of ALL POINTS GLOBAL AND NORWEST RESOURCES Offices in different world cities, and work site location photos and Geological survey-maps. The thirty storey view of Brisbane and its river is breath-taking, but from the lofty POV the city also looks vulnerable, as if the building may be a predator eyeing off its prey. VICKY stands facing the meeting

JOSEPH HAMILTON DEPUTY VICE
PRESIDENT

It's a pleasure to finally meet you VICTORIA. We
were most pleased with your handling of the case
against our fertilizer Subsidiary near Newcastle
and their inadvertent miscalculation about the
damage to the local water supply and soils. Your
savvy and skills have been noticed by Head Office
and we'd like to offer you the job RUPERT already
referenced to you. And we'd also like you to look
at a small accident involving one of our container
ships on the Great Barrier Reef. The new job will
double your current salary. I thought I should ask
you in for a brief belated welcome to the Team and
introduce you to the inner sanctum..

He is about to introduce the other MEN and WOMAN but VICKY
has done her homework and she nods to them one by one and
names them, which further impresses them

VICKY

JAMES CLARKE, CHRISTIAN ABLETT, MARY
ANISTON, AND WALTER CAINE.

They give her a little clap and she makes to depart.

HAMILTON

There's a corporate dinner on Friday night and I'm
letting you know you're very much invited. The
tickets are with my Personal Assistant BRENDA.
She's in the office adjacent to RECEPTION.

#34 INT.ALL POINTS GLOBAL HEAD OFFICE.DAY

A soon as she leaves, HAMILTON starts the OMINOUS prepped film. All eyes are engrossed and watch footage that focuses the company's secret plans for mining and drilling in THE SOUTH PACIFIC, DAINTREE FOREST, THE BARRIER REEF DEVELOPMENTS, the WAYNTON NUCLEAR POWER PLANT AND RAINFOREST VALLEY AND THE OCEAN RIVER.

#35 EXT AFGHANISTAN SEMI DESERT AREA.DAY SUPER PRESENT DAY

WILL and seven other heavily armed S.A.S SOLDIERS reconnoitre a small isolated VILLAGE and its surrounds. It seems normal and quiet but WILL thinks he's spotted a militant hiding near a run-down house.

They send FORWARD SCOUTS from opposite directions but the two SOLDIERS encounter automatic weapons fire near the VILLAGE and WILL and the others advance with COVER FIRE to protect their retreat. One younger SOLDIER is hit in the shoulder and WILL risks everything and races across open GROUND to carry him to safety. In doing so WILL sets off a small anti-personnel MINE which blows off his leg below the knee. His TEAM fight to reach him and one calls in a MISSILE STRIKE THAT SAVES THE DAY. The SOLDIER WILL rescues dies and WILL's close to death as well. FADE TO BLACK

#36 INT.MILITARY HOSPITAL. KABUL. DAY

FADE IN. WILL groggily awakes to see FIVE MEN from his UNIT, staring down at him. He's slurring from the pain killers.

> WILLIAM
> Who let you PROPHYLACTICS out of the holding cells.
> They grin. He'll be alright. He suddenly looks deadly serious Did…did TIM make it?

THEY shake their heads simultaneously and his looks harden. A

NURSE comes with an energy drink he gratefully accepts.

> NURSE CAROL
> MAJOR BAKER's not up to too much excitement
> you guys..

He stares wryly down at the S.O.T.A blade-runner prosthetic leg and foot he now wears from his knee down.

> WILL
> Tell 'em CAROL. Tell 'em I also lost 50% of
> my options for removing land mines from
> AGHANISTAN foot by foot.

The NURSE smiles awkwardly and departs

> ROLY
> I bought you a DVD to watch mate. It seemed
> appropriate.

He passes WILL a copy of "FOOTLOOSE" starring KEVIN BACON and they all laugh. Gallows humour helps keep these GUYS going.

> ROLY
> Anyway, it'll probably grow back WILL.

> TERRY
> Sure: DYNAMIC LIFTER and peeing on your leg
> regularly should do the trick!

> NUGGET
> Yeah and I think on our next visit we'll be able to
> bring some Found Footage with a bit of luck

There's more ironic pseudo laughter.

> JIMMY
> BUT, enough whinging, because you're a million times luckier than our dear departed fellow GRUNT TIM MALONEY. So let's at least toast the brave BASTARD in his absence. RIP TIMMY.

JIMMY produces a six pack of FOSTERS and they all drink to TIMMY's memory.

#37 SUPER:WAYNTON, RAINFOREST VALLEY N.S.W 2019

WILL drives an aging RODEO UTILITY over a bridge off a coastal highway indicating he's passing over OCEAN RIVER and heading towards WAYNTON NORTHERN N.S.W. WILL no longer looks like a SOLDIER. He's more fringe-HIPPIE now and bearded with slightly long hair. From the looks on his face he's been away for years, as some of the country he passes through looks like another kind of WAR ZONE. His face registers a vacant stare.

He pulls over and gets out near an abandoned MINING SITE. There are great craters and it's like a wasteland.

> WILL
> Poor Feller My Country alright! What the HELL's going on here?

#38 EXT/IT COUNTRY HIGHWAY AND LINK ROADS.DAY

Big speeding trucks clog the roads. There's also massive mining equipment and steel built Demountable accommodation located near some of the "still-active" CRATERS, but others look as though they've long been abandoned with no attempt to assist their recovery for land use.

#39 EXT.COUNTRY HIGHWAY TO WAYNTON. DAY

WILL drives towards the outskirts of the beautiful old town, and sees advertisements for ALL POINTS GLOBAL RESOURCES and BIOKRANEK INDUSTRIES with its monster machinery logo reminiscent of an ANCIENT MARINE DINOSAUR, but some local GRAFFITISTS and TAGGERS have drawn death's heads and skulls on cross bones on the billboards, and there's other graffiti near the railway station saying NO FRACKING and NO FOREIGN LAND GRABS FOR AUSTRALIA. WILL drives onto the verge again and walks down to OCEAN RIVER where he sees three teenagers fishing on the bank. The river looks badly polluted.

> WILLIAM
> JESUS, can this be the same mighty river I knew as a kid? G'day GUYS. How are they biting?

> GARY
> Nothing you'd dare to eat MATE.
> KIM (SASSY GIRL)
> Yeah, mostly carp and two-headed eels They all laugh grimly.

> WILL
> Is that right? We used to catch big trout at this patch of the river when I was about your age. We learned to swim around here, as well,

> WILL
> but it looks too bloody dirty for that now. From all the pollution up north in the RAINTREE MINES I guess?

The TEENAGERS look at each other with raised eyebrows and laugh.

> KIM
> NO ONE swims here anymore, and it's not 'cause of the pollution!

WILL's look begs the question.
> GARY
> BULL SHARKS! Lots of them!

WILL's wide-eyed shocked
> KIM
> There's warnings all along the river. I dunno where the one that's supposed to be here's gone though. Probly the sharks pinched it.

> WILL
> Okay, thanks for the heads up, as you TEENAGERS say today. Catch you later

They think his "heads up" is lame as they half watch him limp up the river bank. KIM suddenly points dramatically as some big thing moves near the opposite river bank

#40 EXT/INT THE OUTSKIRTS AND TOWN OF WAYNTON. DAY

WILL drives past his old high school and smiles to himself as he sees kids kicking a football and has a momentary flashback of him and NED kicking to each other.

#41 EXT.MONTAGE OF THE TOWN AND ITS HISTORICAL BUILDINGS.

A SERIES OF DISSOLVES as WILL drives through the timeless streets and classic Federation era houses and earlier workers' cottages of the picturesque old town and most photogenic parts of the river. Across the river he's dismayed to see a mostly ugly new town growing, with new pillar-box apartment buildings.

TRACKING: He drives across the bridge and shakes his head at the ALL POINTS GLOBAL Satellite Development sign. The new club with its myriad poker machines and the "plastic" Italian restaurant car park is full of rev head cars with only a very few a few non yobbo ones. He drives past an expensive looking brothel in this new development and seems stunned as he drives back across the river and out of town to his family's home.

#42 EXT.INT. LONE PINE.BAKER FAMILY HOME PRESENT DAY

WILL idles at the gates to LONE PINE and finally gets out and opens them, drives through, and locks them after him. It's a wonderful heritage-listed mid-19th century building. He closes his eyes for a few seconds and has a flashback memory as he stands there

EXT/INT FLASHBACK MEMORY OF LONE PINE IN THE BROTHERS' YOUTH

IN FLEETING FLASHBACK: WILL and NED are seen riding their HORSES through the gates, admiring the homestead and looking proudly at their home and farm. He sees flash images of them working the PROPERTY and it looks a special place.

#43 EXT. LONE PINE. DAY

He gets back into the car and follows the winding gravel road past the stables, barn, beautiful garden and swimming pool to the house. An old fashioned septuagenarian WOMAN comes out and they hug each other, having been separated for a decade.

> EDITH BAKER
> Oh WILL it's fantastic to see you. Your DAD's had a few turns since last you saw him. These last ten years have been particularly stressful for him and the death - or the disappearance, of your BROTHER - nearly killed him. He'll never fully get over it.

WILL puts his arm around EDITH. They go into the house and she can't stop crying.

#44 INT. LONE PINE HOMESTEAD. NIGHT

Inside time's stood still. It's old world ENGLAND and AUSTRALIA furniture with paintings of animals by STUBBS and others as well as JOHN GLOVER landscapes, as well as family PORTRAITS, world furniture. The new LED TV and DVD player looks strangely out of place.His FATHER JOSEPH is dozing in a comfortable old leather chair with a book in his lap. EDITH touches his shoulder gently and wakes him.

> EDITH BAKER
> Wakey-wakey, FARMER BOY. You have a visitor.

The SLEEPER slowly opens his eyes and smiles. Tears well in his eyes as he stands and hugs his son and weeps from happiness.

> JOSEPH BAKER
> So good... Ah, WILL! Lost track of time there...
> How long this time son? You're not going back to
> fight in VIETNAM are you...

WILL glances at his MOTHER. JOSEPH's memory's a worry.

> EDITH
> VIETNAM ended 40 years ago Love. WILL fought
> in AGHANISTAN and IRAQ.

> JOSEPH
> Why in GOD's name would AUSTRALIANS be
> fighting in those bloody countries?

>   WILL
> For OIL and UNITED NATIONS B/S conscience
> pretence and Political BROWNIE POINTS, DAD.
> No more wars for me though. I'm back for good
> now and I won't leave you and MUM again.

They both look very happy and relieved at this news.

>   WILLIAM
> You'll have to give me a crash course in the fine
> points of farming in the modern era though,
> because I've forgotten almost everything I ever
> learned.

The old man is delighted.

>   JOSEPH BAKER
> The boy will be hungry. Have we got any leftover
> roast EDITH? We've got some hired help these
> days WILL - DOREEN'S a full time cook and
> cleans, some student travellers arelooking after
> the garden, milking cows..mowing and..

>   EDITH
> They're hard workers all, WILL and there's a
> couple of clever young TAMWORTH lads been
> Managing the place and we just keep a general eye
> on them. Graduates of your old school YANCO
> AGRICULTURAL COLLEGE. It's all a big help.

>   WILL
> I can see that. I hope they'll leave me something
> to do.

>   EDITH
> You hungry WILL? I could rustle up some leftovers
> or a pizza.

His DAD's almost asleep in his chair again.

> WILL
> No, thanks MUM. Dad's out to it (NODS AT DAD) and you won't be long after. I might drop into the WAYNTON ARMS and have a few beers. Catch up with some old mates and learn what I'm up against starting over,

> EDITH BAKER
> You'll find there's another kind of battle going on in WAYNTON WILL. And not just here. Australia's in a fight for its very future. WAYNTON's going to be a symbolic battleground, mark my words! We've NEVER confronted these kinds of ruthless people in our everyday lives before. They're evil white collar CRIMINALS WILL. And it seems there's an Army of them

> WILL (GOBSMACKED)
> MUM? You sound like a loopy left wing radical. What ruthless people?

> EDITH
> Politicians, big companies, Australian Traitors. They're selling out our CHILDREN'S and their CHILDREN'S futures Pet. All for their greed. Scum! Every one of them. They say MC DOUGALL MINING, NORDWEST RESOURCES and ALL POINTS GLOBAL are the main culprits but DAVE FINGLETON up RAINTREE WAY claims this has the shady signature of BIO-KRANEK written all over it.

WILL knows how sharp she is and he's stunned at this last mention.

> WILL
> FINGLETON really said that?
> BIO-KRANEK INTERNATIONAL? JESUS, IF
> SATAN HAD GONE INTO BUSINESS INSTEAD

> WILL
> OF JUST TRYING TO PISS OFF GOD, HE
> WOULD HAVE MADE HIMSELF CEO OF
> BIOKRANEK MULTINATIONAL.

EDITH nods grimly and he takes full stock of this information and hugs her before heading out into a rainy night

#45 EXT/INT. OCEAN RIVER HOTEL WAYNTON HOTEL. NIGHT

WILL angle parks his old UTE outside the hotel, whose legend reads: WAYNTON RIVER OCEAN HOTEL 1847. When he enters, the crowded bar he's happy to recognize so many familiar faces. There's a band setting up to play, lots of past friends, TEACHERS and fellow FARMERS greet him. They all know he's been away and at least a dozen males and females call out greetings or wave to him and offer him a beer.

Few anywhere would have WILL's standing, respect and popularity and he seems genuinely surprised. There's even a uniformed cop drinking a squash among the well-wishers. The CHOIR BOYS' classic "RUN TO PARADISE" is playing on the Juke Box as a middle-aged and greying Cow Cocky in R.M Williams cream trousers and riding boots and wide-brimmed hat brings him a beer.

> COW COCKY 1
> WILL BAKER how the hell are yer? We all heard
> you'd been fighting towel-heads in HELLMUND
> PROVINCE. HELL. sounds
> like an appropriate name.

                    WILL
They're lethal and fearless FIGHTERS. We always
respected their bravery.

                    COW COCKY 1
          HELLMUND'S IRAQ..yeah?

A LOCAL in torn jeans and a sleeveless football jumper buts in..
                    BLUEY
HELLMUND'S AFGHANISTAN actually. In the
S.A.S WILL was: The Real deal. You're a credit to
the WAYNTON GOANNAS

                    WILL.
And to the town. Let's drink a toast to this bastard..
and to his brother NED, who was lost to us.! To
the BAKER BOYS, and so say all of us.

                    ALL
To the BAKER BROTHERS!

Several of them instinctively look down at his leg even though
he's wearing jeans. He doesn't keep them in suspense and lifts the
bottom of his jeans leg to show the futuristic steel and titanium
contraption.

All are quiet for a second but he fixes that.
                    WILL
It's a State of the Art JAPANESE high tech foot. It
gets me all the FM RADIO stations and can make
a six inch dent in the backside of anyone who
pisses me off.

The awkwardness diminishes. Most smile in empathy.

#46 INT. WAYNTON ARMS PUB BISTRO. PRESENT DAY 2019

The Bistro is one of WAYNTON's other pubs. It is upmarket for a country town and the Mayor brings in three important looking Chinese businessmen for a meal. The bistro has adjoining booths and they sit at a table next to one with two Caucasian Australians drinking heavily.

The CHINESE businessmen are all self-important and talk in MANADARIN in fairly loud voices, among the loud hubbub in the Bistro. One of the AUSTRALIAN MEN visits the kitchen and comes back with its CHINESE AUSTRALIAN RESTAURATEUR/ CHEF, whom he seats at their table without the adjoining group's noticing him. They instruct him to listen in and take notes. The Asian BUSINESSMEN are indiscreet in their native MANDARIN and show contempt for the MAYOR by rarely speaking English. After they finish and leave the restaurant the other two locals look to the chef wide-eyed.

> ROBBIE
> Wow! Were they talking your kind of CHINESE,
> PHILLIP? Is it CANTONESE you speak?

> PHILLIP WONG
> I'm not just a short order cook, MATE. I've got
> a degree in Business Studies from MONASH and
> I speak HOKKIENESE, CANTONESE and even
> some KOREAN and JAPANESE. Funnily enough,
> though, I'm also fluent in MANDARIN, which is
> what those arrogant dickheads spoke

The other two listen excitedly, hungry to learn what was said, but all three of them are "piss" takers and wary of each other.

> BEN
> What can you tell us PHIL?

PHILLIP WONG
Well for starters, all three are off the charts SMUG
BUGGERS.

BEN
And? What else?

PHILLIP
Well, they think our esteemed MAYOR is a greedy
fuck wit: and probably a transvestite to boot.

ROBBIE (SHRUGGING INDIFFERENTLY)
Yeah! What else?
PHILLIP WONG
And they think themselves so superior they
completely dismissed all the people in this town
as dumb HICKS and RHUBS.

ROBBIE
Arrogant twats!

PHILLIP does a visible rethink and keeps what the visitors said to
himself though, and fibs.

PHILLIP
They're thinking of building some COLLEGE here
for ASIAN STUDENTS.

BEN
Is that all? Well we don't need that do we?

PHILLIP
I've gotta get back to my kitchen.

SUPER: PRESENT DAY.TOWNSVILLE NORTH QUEENSLAND

#47 EXT. TROPICAL NORTH QUEENSLAND ATHLETIC PARK & BEACH. 2017

An idyllic AUSTRALIAN summer's day in a garden suburb. A kids' little ATHLETIC carnival is in progress. A beautiful white beach, with groves of palm trees can be seen in the deep background. A fat MAN with a fishing rod crosses the road and disappears into the palms.

#48 INT.EXCELLENT GARAGE GYM ADJACENT TO ATHLETICS FIELD

VICKY and two other very fit looking young WOMEN are training in a well-appointed Garage GYM with a fighting ring and all the training gear set up. VICKY"s wearing head gear and mouth-guard and sparring and kick boxing in the ring with a powerful looking SENSAI(NICK PELLE, 38)and they're really going at it. VICKY 's elusive and fast with her fists and feet and giving as good as she gets. JOANNA (now in her late forties) arrives to watch. She watches her daughter with pride.

> JOANNA
> Come on VICKY. Put him to sleep.

The SPARRING PAIR and the other two FIGHT-STUDENTS laugh at her interjection.

VICKY looks to have real potential as an MEA fighter. She suddenly ducks under NICK'S right cross, grabs his arm, brings him to the canvas and grabs his wrist in a submission hold. The others clap as NICK climbs to his feet.

> NICK
> Hey JOANNA. Glad you could make it!

JOANNA
Looks like I arrived just in time to save you from a shellacking. She's improving, yeah.

NICK (LAUGHING)
Yeah, you could say that! And she's brainy as well!

PAN out from the gym and past the Athletics
Field to the palm trees and a picturesque strip of white beach.
Beyond the beach is the PACIFIC OCEAN. ZOOM TO:

#49 EXT. TROPICAL NORTH QUEENSLAND BEACH. DAY

Seen from behind, a portly shirtless MAN, in tropical- swimming-trunks, carries a fishing-rod and a keep-net and guzzles a can of beer as he walks a path leading through palms to a beach. As he walks he throws the can at a garbage bin on the edge of the sand. He totally misses the bin and almost hits a scavenging rat feeding on some chips some other litterer has thrown. He watches the rat scurry off into the foliage and wanders toward the lapping waters, wading in up to his knees.

FROM UNDERWATER POV TO: A lethal STONE FISH is MOVING over some coral towards his vulnerable-looking foot Next, he casts his fishing rod toward deeper-water and immediately gets a bite. SLOWMO UNDERWATER POV AS HE Lifts his foot and it comes down on the stonefish. He lets out an almighty scream of pain

FISHERMAN
Aargh! Ohh God! Help! Help me..!
He suddenly clutches his heart and disappears under water

#50 - 51 EXT. TOWNSVILLE BEACH.DAY

A middle aged WOMAN abruptly emerges from the palms and jogs onto the beach with her DOG. She hurls a tennis-ball and the animal rushes after it but stops abruptly when the ball goes into the water. It starts growling as it stares out at the place where the FISHERMAN had just been wading. The MAN has disappeared without a trace.

#52 EXT. SLOOP SOUTH PACIFIC.PRESENT: 2019

Several dissolves show a sleek old yacht that's sailing through Pacific expanses and archipelagos. On deck are PAT and Rita and MAI(20-22) lounging on the deck drinking and smoking dope. Then there's Colin, a 20 year solid Pakeha MALE in the wheelhouse steering the boat.

Another man, an overweight half MAORI struggles up off the deck looking drunk. He scans the horizon through binoculars and focuses on one picturesque island.

> PAT
> That's the one BRO! Let's weigh anchor and stay on that island for a day or so before we head for NEW CALEDONIA! We can spear fish and catch dinner in the lagoon and sleep on the beach. Collect some coconut milk to add to those bottles of KAHLUA!

The others are all for this suggestion and give him a cheer as the stand and ready to sail in over the reef.

#53 EXT. CORAL ATOLL DAY.

JON RANDALL trails his hand in the azure water as the MOONGLIDER coasts in over the coral. On an impulse he leaps into the water as soon as they traverse the razor sharpness. The others drop anchor, get into a dingy and set out for the shore.

JON
It's as warm as a bath you guys!

He free-styles after the dinghy towards the beach that bounds a football field-sized island. They're all yelling and carrying on as they set out to explore the tiny island. JON squats under a coconut palm to empty the water from his gym shoes that he's collected on the short swim.

RITA
I wouldn't sit under that tree for too long JOHNNY RANDALL. Lots of people get killed every year when coconuts drop on their heads: I'm not joking!

He leaps up and bounds after the others as they disappear into the undergrowth.

After collecting some wild bananas and paw paws in the canvas bags they have, they scale a little volcanic outcrop. They study the lush trees and dense undergrowth creep up to the narrow beach.

COLIN
MAI and I reckon we need to spread out and see what other food we can find. Might even be some wild pigs!

RITA
You'll be the one who has to kill it if we find one. I hate killing things.

PAT
I will: I'll do it. I've killed plenty of 'em.

The others look at him as if they have no idea who he really is. COLIN suddenly produces an old handgun and grins.

> MAI
> Why have you brought that?

> COLIN
> Man I wasn't headin' into the wild ocean without
> some kind of protection!

JON'S scouting ahead and is stunned to find the entrance to what looks like a cave, partly hidden by some foliage.

> JON
> Avast me hearties: Look what I found: a bloody
> PIRATES' cave aargh!

They clear plant debris from the entrance but seem reluctant to enter. PAT produces a torch and picks up a stick and goes in.

#54 INT. CAVE ON PACIFIC ATOLL. DAY

It's dark inside. The others follow with more torches. They discern something propped against the back wall of the cave.

> COLIN
> Oh crap! Is that what I think it is?

They discover a male skeleton in rotting shorts, with a rotting bandage round its lower skeletal leg. Nearby is an old bag, which they retrieve. They photograph the scene with their Mobiles.

#55 INT MOORED MOON-GLIDER SLOOP. INTERIOR CORAL REEF.NIGHT

Back inside the cabin they examine the numerous contents of the bag and do Internet scans.

                    MAI
I'm sure I've heard that name NED BAKER. This
undeveloped film and old cassette recordings look
important.

                    PAT
Hey, maybe there's a reward

                    MAI
I'm getting a bad feeling about this. There's
something definitely doesn't add up about how
and why he died and especially where he died.
Looking at him it wasn't old age that killed him.

                    COLIN
Maybe he was accidentally marooned like Tom
Hanks in that movie. So where's WILSON?

                    MAI
We have to take part of the skeleton back with us:
it'll be needed for DNA testing!

The others look at her as if she's a Brainiac.

              JON (GOOGLING NED)
Eureka! Found it! Yes, bad juju did happen to NED
- let's call him BONES - BAKER - the skeleton guy.

They all hang on his words

He was a Queensland Corporate LAWYER who
went missing on a 20 metre ketch called BIG SKY
in 1995 along
with six environmental activists from six different
countries. They were

> JON

studying the effects of nuclear fallout in French Polynesia though some investigative Journalist claimed they had secretly gone to MORUROA ATOLL to demonstrate against last FRENCH Nuclear Tests as well.

The others crowd around and read the entries

> MAI

"Courier Mail" Journalist JOANNA DANIELS even claimed they could have been killed by mercenaries or a sleeper cell of French DGSE agents. Says here she was NED's pregnant lover but got sick and remained in NOUMEA. All the crew were presumed dead.

> JON

DANIELS is now a freelance Journo and part time lecturer in TOWNSVILLE!

A light goes on in PAT's opportunistic brain.

> PAT

Guaranteed all this stuff is worth something to somebody CUZ. The mother of his CHILD would also want to bury his bones. And "probly" pay us for that film stuff shit. I'm guessin' it'd be worth developin'. How do we all feel about phonin' A CURRENT AFFAIR and soundin' out about a reward. There's gotta be a hundred grand in this for us. Maybe more!

MAI and JON's looks say they could ask three times that. The other two can already see dollar signs in each other's eyes.

MAI
Be that as it may, his PARTNER and MOTHER
of his DAUGHTER would rightly have first dibs
I think.
And definitely some Legal claims. Maybe
SENTINEL does too.

RITA
This'll be tough for his family!

JON
And probably a huge relief as well! And you're
right PAT - we'd still be justified in asking for some
reward.

JON
Not from those mainstream TV JOURNO vultures
though! Let's telephone her and ask for $50 K! Ten
grand each is a good little earner and also the right
thing to do!

Only PAT looks ticked off, as he wants more!
We need fuel and some caulking repairs so how
about we sail to NOUMEA first and make the call
to JO DANIELS from there.

They're almost all on the same page now.
But we have to play it cool from now on. If the
authorities in Noumea get wind of it they might
confiscate it all and claim the reward themselves.

Only MAI has also considered this possibility..
MAI
Yeah we have to be really careful. Record this exact
location and only take his teeth and some hair.

PAT and RITA exchange a sly dismissive suggesting they think
she's a power-freak.

#56 EXT/INT MARINA OUTSIDE NOUMEA.MORNING

JON and MAI get a signal on her Mobile and they make the call. The other three go to a restaurant for a late lunch.

#57 INT.JOANNA'S HOUSE QUEENSLAND.MORNING

JOANNA and VICKY are playing Scrabble when the phone rings. JOANNA's DEVASTATED. Her hand is shaking as she writes details.

> JOANNA
> And..how can you be absolutely sure it's him. Yes, for a DNA. At least read one of the letters addressed to me. His nickname for me would prove it.

She gasps and puts her hand over her mouth as she listens

> Really? It says JODIE? Yes! Yes! I'll get the first plane to NOUMEA - tomorrow if possible. Sorry, how much did you say? Erm, yes of course I understand you COULD likely sell it to a TV Network. But he was my PARTNER and I now have a grown DAUGHTER by him. We were going to get married, so I hope you see why.... Yes, yes $50 thousand is..is do able! Yes, we can do that amount. And Please, please, please, do not contact another living soul about this. I'll hopefully meet you at your hotel sometime tomorrow or the day after at the latest. Thank you...

She fights shock and grief.

VICKY's tearful with anticipation.

JOANNA DANIELS (LOOKING FAINT)
Oh..VICKY! Darling (PAUSE) NED, your Dad..
they've found his body LOVE
She starts to weep and hugs her daughter.
We'll finally be able to bury him and honour his
memory.

VICKY's beset by conflicting emotions. They're both tearful.
JOANNA makes other calls.

#58 INT. JOANNA'S HOUSE DAY

Several MEN and WOMEN from SENTINEL are in discussion in
the lounge room. JOANNA's making notes in a little black book.

JOANNA
I've thought about it and you should stay here in
TOWNSVILLE VICKY.

SIMON
SENTINEL will pay the reward money. I've
booked three tickets to NOUMEA via BRISBANE
early in the morning. I can't go of course as I'm on
the French Government's persona non grata list.

JOANNA
VICKY'S UNCLE WILL's driving here tonight
from Northern N.S.W after I told him what's
happened.
SENTINEL said they already have an ex
commando named BRENDAN, who works with
them sometimes. He and WILL make two GUYS
with the right stuff to afford me proper protection.

VICKY
Protection! What the heck are you talking about
MUM?

                    JOANNA
Things were very volatile there not so long ago -
between the indigenous

                    JOANNA
KANAKS and the FRENCH and GERMAN
and other EUROPEAN SETTLERS..and the so
called PIED NOIRES hard line patriotic French
military VETERANS who settled there.. PARIS
sent thousands of SOLDIERS there to prevent a
possible civil war. Quite a lot were killed, and many
indigenes want independence. It still warrants
extreme caution going in with what I'm hoping to
retrieve.
VICKY, some conspiracy theorists still claim the
BIG SKY was sabotaged or attacked by some right
wing EXTREMISTS from there or pro FRENCH
PARAMILITARIES. Whoever it was though
this discovery of your Dad's body, his papers
and undeveloped films might prove incendiary
politically! It needs secure processing, evaluation
and production for public evaluation.

VICKY stares into the garden, in a state of emotional numbness.

                    VICKY
I can't get my head around this MUM. It's terrible
sad and horrible at the same time! What will it
mean for our lives?

                    JOANNA
I'm afraid we'll need to be prepared for less privacy
in our lives. At least for a while.

#59 EXT.NOUMEA AIRPORT. DAY

MONTAGE: JOANNA and WILL BAKER, (now 48) and BRENDAN SNOW walk through the airport doors and get in a taxi. MOVING: Their taxi cruises through scattered jungle and then they drive through interesting parts of the city.

#60 INT. HOTEL REIRAKI.RESTAURANT AND BAR. DAY

WILL, JOANNA AND BRENDAN sit around a table in the empty bar with RITA, COLIN, MAI and JON. The other patrons sit outside in the sun.

> JOANNA
> Well? Where is it? And where the Hell is….

THE KIWIS look at each other sheepishly (They're Kiwis).

> MAI
> Actually..we've struck a glitch

JOANNA's look makes them really uncomfortable.

> MAI
> The thing is, yesterday, we went to a pub off the main street; and some GENDARMES saw our friend PAT looking a bit worse for wear, and ..

WILL and BRENDAN look increasingly frustrated.

> BRENDAN
> Please - while we're still young! So they confronted this PAT? And he was legless and abusive? Right?

> MAI
> More like chatty and cheerful

                    WILLIAM
And he …resisted arrest?

                    MAI (STRESSED AND SHRUGGING)
He… had some Marijuana on him. None of
us knew about it. And, he erm, laughed at a
GENDARME. They roughed him up..

JOANNA, WILL and BRENDAN are gobsmacked.
                    WILL
This just gets better and better. So filling in the rest
of the dots:
the authorities then examined your boat and
turned it over expecting to find more marijuana,
impounded the suspicious bag you found, and
took it and your EINSTEIN mate to the central
lock up for questioning and to sober up? Is that
right?

Their looks confirm his fears. MAI nods in humiliation and looks
down at the floor

                    BRENDAN
So how much dope DID the Dope have on him?

She shows a tiny space between her thumb and forefinger.
BRENDAN pats JOANNA'S arm to comfort her. WILLIAM notices
his uninvited familiarity and takes a mental note. He seems vaguely
suspicious of BRENDAN

                    BRENDAN
It doesn't sound like this PAT can be trusted not to
spill the beans

                    MAI
He's RITA's cousin and kind of invited himself
along on our trip. None of us liked him much as
he's sometimes aggressive as well as being a loud
mouth and a heavy drinker.

                    RITA

He does have some good qualities MAI. His DAD
used to beat up on him and his MUM. His Dad
ended up in gaol. A lot of kids wouldn't deal well
with that.

                    WILL

Okay, this is how we play it: RITA and I will go
to the Gendarmerie. If the Cops had known what
they had though, you'd all be in holding cells right
now. I'll pretend to be a friend of PAT'S father,
"who's sick" back in ..

                    RITA

He's in WELLINGTON

                    WILL

Sure! You're up to this RITA? Give me the skinny
on PAT on the way there.

#61 INT.GENDARMERIE. DAY

WILL and RITA sit in an office across from a mid-rank Gendarme
officer. WILL's making headway, through politeness and military
experience. He sees NED's bag on the floor. The officer is impressed
with WILLIAM'S French and his confidence. He doesn't object
when WILL pushes an unmarked envelope across the table. It's
several thousand dollars and it gets the desired result. When a
chastened and slightly dishevelled PAT is brought in WILLIAM
addresses him briefly as a cranky parent might.

                    WILLIAM

Well bloody done PAT. Bien fait DINGO
The FRENCH OFFICER laughs at his calling PAT
DINGO, who is "GOOFY" from DISNEY comics
for FRANCOPHONES

> WILL
> I was in Sydney and your Dad asked me to sort
> this out.
> The very generous LIEUTENANT LAFITTE here
> has agreed to let you off with a warning, but you
> and your crew need to depart this island within
> the week. Understood?

PAT'S bewildered but is wise enough to play along And I now I suggest you that you thank the LIEUTENANT and we'll be on our way.

> PAT (CONTRITE AND NERVOUS)
> Um, Merci Monsewer. Um, thank you for letting
> me go. I'm very sorry.

The FRENCHMAN nods okay, shakes PAT'S hand and WILLIAM'S hand and gets NED'S bag for him.

#61B INT. KIWIS' HOTEL ROOM. DAY

Everyone's relieved when they return. RITA opens some champagne. JOANNA nods towards the bathroom and she and WILLIAM take the mystery bag to the bathroom to check it.

#62 INT. BATHROOM. DAY

They examine letters, cassettes and photos. Most are for JO, one's addressed to WILL and one to VICKY. JO reads two short letters in a whisper: they're dynamite! The cassettes and the undeveloped film alarms them.

#63 INT. DINING-ROOM&LOUNGE OF THE HOTEL SUITE. EVENING

WILL gives the Kiwis their $50K reward in cash and their faces light up. JON hands JOANNA a piece of paper.

> JON
> Those are the coordinates of where we found the deceased..erm, your former partner. We didn't think it safe or right for us to disturb the remains.

JO's grateful

> WILL
> Okay you young Kiwis, we're booked to fly out to Sydney tomorrow morning, and I've booked PAT on a flight to Wellington at 11.30 A.M

PAT'S ALTERNATELY DEFLATED AND ANGRY. HIS COMPANIONS IGNORE HIM

> WILL
> As for the rest of you, we believe you need to sail out tomorrow, as well. Get well away from French Polynesia.

They agree with this suggestion.

> BRENDAN
> And never mention this to anyone. As for you PAT: no more bloody pubs! Stay here till the taxi we booked picks you up in the morning to take you to the airport.

He eyeballs PAT, who avoids his glare. WILL sees he's more defiant and indignant than contrite. WILL signals MAI with a "Phone me, if" gesture and the threesome leave the hotel.

#64 INT.HOTEL KIWIS' ROOM. NIGHT

> RITA
> Okay, celebration time!
> She opens 2 bottles of champagne to the approval
> of all and counts out her money again

> PAT (SCOFFING IT LIKE IT'S LEMONADE)
> This is horse shit you know! We could've got much
> more than $10 K each. An' I ain't takin orders or
> advice from that arrogant prick neither. He can't
> make me fly home.

> JON
> He saved your crazy arse tonight and got you out
> of a very bad place. Who carries grass around a
> port chock full of cops? And you do need to fly
> home because that's my uncle Paul's boat, and
> I'm not prepared to risk your risky behaviour any
> longer? You're off the crew!

> PAT
> You're full of IT! Fuck all of you..

Only RITA's supportive - until PAT skols almost half a bottle of champagne and strides out, slamming the door after him.

> MAI
> He's in no fit state to be out. I'm phoning WILL.

> JON (NODDING)
> He can't take advice. We need to pack and sail out
> of here at first light: Agreed?

They do. MAI sees the urgency and makes a call.

#65 EXT. STREETS OF NOUMEA LATE AT NIGHT

PAT's wandering aimlessly with a long neck bottle of beer and being a public nuisance along with several drunken islanders. A group of laughing FRENCH FOREIGN LEGIONAIRES lounge and spar outside a seedy-looking bar called BAR PIGALLE. There are also a few youngish KANAK prostitutes trying to entice them into a neon-lit annexe.

#66 PAT wanders in and is soon accosted by a sultry little PROSTITUTE in a revealing outfit. When he offers to buy her a drink, she sees his open wallet and attaches to him like a remora fish. She waves to a nearby table of 5 SOLDIERS in civvies drinking heavily with two hard muscular older MEN, to whom the SOLDIERS show real deference. A closer view shows it's CLAUDE and JEAN LUC from the earlier funeral.

CLAUDE wears an old short sleeved COLOUCHE (past popular comedian) tee shirt which show off crossbow tattoos on each of his impressive biceps. JEAN LUC is much more low-key and hides his formidable physicality.

When PAT buys a round for them all he's their new best friend though they're clearly having "a lend" of him. Soon he's drinking strong PELFORTH BRUN beers with them and spending his money freely. His stash is not lost on the VETERANS as he shouts drinks for his new "best friends". At this point WILL wanders in and takes in the situation instantly. He buys two jugs of beer and approaches the table. He recognizes the "ELDERS" as fellow VETS, and they him. They also note his limp. The stakes are changing.

> WILL (NODDING TO SOLDIERS)
> Bonsoir Messieurs! So, PAT, you found another drinking spot. I thought I'd come and check you're okay.

PAT flushes: he knows he's in trouble. JEAN LUC observes and he and WILLIAM are circumspect about each other

> JEAN LUC
> Your "son" ..

> WILLIAM (CORRECTING)
> An old friend's son

> JEAN LUC
> He has been enjoying himself and been generous to us. Come join us MONSIEUR..erm

> WILL
> WILLIAM: GUILLAUME to you..

WILL and JEAN LUC size each other up.
> JEAN LUC
> You speak FRENCH? Tres bien. I am JEAN LUC and this is CLAUDE ..these young guns are DAVIDE, MICHEL, RAOUL and MARC, soldiers all. And you too I think my friend?

WILLIAM shakes LEAN LUC'S hand and they are a match for strength. The Frenchman sees WILL glance at his half hidden crossbow tattoo on his upper arm.

> WILL
> Special Forces? Legion D'ETRANGERS..Foreign Legion?

> JEAN LUC
> Close enough. And you? IRAQ, right?

> WILL
> In the Ball park…!

They both laugh out loud at their mutually evasive word-fencing. They seem to own up to some of the B.S Of the past

> WILLIAM
> Game of Pool? Twenty francs a game?

JEAN LUC laughs again and they head for the table. They have an easy affinity and WILL judges it the right move.

#67 INT.PAT AND THE SOLDIERS' TABLE.FLEUR DE LYS CLUB. NIGHT

CLAUDE pours them all beers from the huge jug WILL brought. HE and the younger soldiers are almost wasted but at the table JEAN LUC drinks on imperviously. Though increasingly cheerful drunks, the younger men urge CLAUDE to share some stories. Although out of earshot LEAN LUC warns him with an admonishing eyebrow.

> CLAUDE (VERY DRUNK AND LAUGHING)
> Alors! I think I hear a KIWI accent from PAT?
> Baa! It means "hello" IN KIWI non?

> PAT
> Very funny KERMIT

> CLAUDE
> I am CLAUDE. Who is KERMIT?

WILL puts his drink on the table and shakes his head at PAT as if he's demented.

> PAT
> KERMIT is a Frog! The boyfriend of MISS PIGGY
> in the MUPPETS.

CLAUDE smiles wryly.

CLAUDE

NEW ZEALAND is also ze land of Les Ballcks! Ze mighty All Blacks, oui!

All drink a toast to the All Blacks. The soldiers start demanding Old School stories from CLAUDE .

CLAUDE (IN FRENCH WITH SUBTITLES)

Ah in ze Glory days of the Legion we were formidAble, and before us, those in AFRIQUE, ALGIERS and INDOCHINE..

The troops were much tougher than today's Namby Pambies. In the Legion MUSEUM in PARIS the most revered object is from 1836. In MEXICO against the same Generale SANTA ANNA who killed DAVY CROCKETT and many others at the ALAMO. Can you guess what that near holy object is, PAT?

PAT

How the fuck would I know? Is it a red white and blue-coloured condom?

His joke doesn't go down well. PAT gets the message.

CLAUDE

Ton geule (animal mouth) the most valuable memoir in the Miltary Museum is a wooden hand and it belonged to a fearless Legionary captain whose men were massively outnumbered and massacred by the Mexican Army. As the last man standing he charged the thousands in the Mexican army and left his name to Legend.

Behind his back the SOLDIERS suggest he exaggerates. WILL signals PAT it's time to leave. PAT avoids eye contact. Another slightly familiar understated hard man in a lightweight suit with thinning WHITE hair enters. He stands at the end of the bar and orders a drink. He's the MAN seen at GEORGE's funeral. He nods at JEAN LUC, who slowly wanders over to the bar. WILL notes J.LUC'S slight deference to the man.

>   CLAUDE
> I can tell you one great true story if I'm quick …
> He glances at JEAN LUC as if he's about to tell a
> risky tale It's about how free and how wild we
> were back in the 1970's - when I was the age you
> all are now. JEAN LUC and I were training for
> COMMANDOS at the secret Frogman base in
> ASPRETTO CORSICA. We did as we pleased
> down there. Corsican WOMEN on tap, we didn't
> pay for many drinks or meals at restaurants either,
> got in fights with locals. You know what young
> BUCKS get up to..

He winks at the awed young men and suddenly lets out a hacking cough suggesting serious illness. WILLIAM knows there'll be trouble if JEAN LUC hears CLAUDE'S story. JEAN LUC and the suited man converse intently and JEAN LUC's taking notes.

>   CLAUDE
> Though there was one there in Corsica who decided
> to play the LONE RANGER: a MAGISTRATE
> whose name I forget: Well he complained about
> us in the newspaper. Tried to get the authorities
> to punish us. So, you know what JEAN LUC and
> GEORGE and I did...

They all hang on his words as he tells the story and it plays out audio visually "in his memory LIKE A PHOTOGRAPHIC ANIMATION

He had Political ambitions you see, and demanded a Government inquiry into the ASPRETTO Base. He was smug and needed a lesson we thought. So he went to dinner one night at a nice restaurant, drove home in his nice car to their nice house, bid the nice

> CLAUDE
> young baby sitter good night, kissed his nice sleeping child and went to bed and fucked his nice sexy wife till they fell into a nice deep sleep. Then we paid them a surprise visit: wearing balaclavas and carrying magnums, as was the fashion at the time.

> YOUNG SOLDIER GASTON (GASPING)
> And..and what happened next?

> CLAUDE (LAUGHING)
> Well the smart MAGISTRATE was not so smart after that because the next morning he awoke freezing his balls off: In a rubber dinghy! In the middle of the fucking MEDITERRANEAN SEA.

His listeners are stunned. They all know it's a true story.

> CLAUDE
> He was rescued of course. It was a warning but it was a mistake because the three of us ended up posted to very dangerous jobs with the FORCE DU FRAPPE Nuclear Tests on MORUROA, with 5 days monthly leave in PAPEETE!
> He places his index finger on his lips in a shhh sign and whispers That's where GEORGE and I got MORUROA LEUKEMIA as they call it: Our cancers.

One of the SOLDIERS quietly whistles at his amazing story.

CLAUDE(SOBERING UP SUDDENLY)
Best don't repeat that story. Just a Soldier's tale.
We were young and stupid. Now those times have
gone

PAT intuits WILL'S mood and when WILL rolls his eyes towards
the door he stands up and prepares to go.

WILL (YAWNING AND SALUTING THEM)
Okay everybody, merci et bonsoir..erm, goodnight

Two SOLDIERS laugh and return WILLIAM'S salute and the others
nod and pour more drinks.

WILLIAM (WHISPERING TO PAT)
Walk at normal pace and nod good night to JEAN
LUC but not to the Suit. Don't look back and keep
going straight out.

JEAN LUC watches them go with a slightly concerned look
WILLIAM notes the suspicious looks the SUIT gives them.

#68 EXT/INT. STREET NOUMEA STREET. NIGHT

They enter a taxi at the KIWIS' hotel.

WILLIAM
Get your suitcase PAT. You're not leaving my sight
till I get you on that plane tomorrow morning.

#69 INT/EXT.NOUMEA. DAY

JOANNA, BRENDAN, WILLIAM and PAT exit a taxi at the airport.
PAT looks extremely angry.

#70 INT. EXT. AIRPORT DEPARTURE LOUNGE NOUMEA. DAY

WILL clutches NED's bag as if it's a King's ransom. The Sydney plane leaves half an hour earlier than the Auckland plane. JOANNA and BRENDAN watch WILL lecturing PAT until their boarding call. WILL is the last to board and he waves back at the viewing deck but as he's about to enter the jet, PAT gives him the finger sign and heads back into the lounge for the exit.

#71 INT.SYDNEY BOUND PLANE.

> WILLIAM (IN VEILED FURY)
> The little fucker! Jesus but that KID's one very temporary KIWI. He could make big problems for us.

> JOANNA (CONCERNED)
> God I hope not. I wonder if he'll leave with his friends.

#72 EXT.NOUMEA MARINA AND PORT AREA. DAY

PAT is a dejected figure wandering round the marina. He has a sad, self-recriminating look as he stares out to sea. He counts his money and heads to a decent hotel with his suitcase.

#73 EXT/INT.BAR PIGALLE. DAY

CLAUDE and JEAN LUC and "the suit" are there again. They're friendly and welcoming, which he's in need of.

> CLAUDE
> Ha! Ca va! It's our NOUVELLE ZEALAND friend PAT with the fat wallet!

JEAN LUC looks very concerned to see PAT and studies "the suit" as if he might wish PAT harm

PAT

Bonjour to you blokes. Can I get youse a drink. I know it's really early...

CLAUDE

Never early too much for us. But this round on moi. Is my bar after all! Where is your friend from last night? GUILLAUME..I thought he fly back with you to Sydney?

PAT

WILLIAM's not my bloody friend. I only met him yesterday. My actual friends sailed away and left me.

CLAUDE and JEAN LUC LUC are genuinely sorry – and concerned- for him..like fathers with a difficult son. CLAUDE brings him a jug of PELFORTH BRUN "as a gift" and PAT's happy again.

JEAN LUC

PAT, this is our friend MICHAEL ARLINGTON. He's an international BUSINESSMAN.

CLAUDE

Who is GUILLAUME then? And why TOUS LE MONDE.erm, everyone everyone leave NOUMEA so quick?

JEAN LUC has guessed PAT'S in trouble and wants to shut up CLAUDE and PAT before ARLINGTON gets at him

PAT(SUDDENLY APPREHENSIVE AND EVASIVE)

I'm not supposed to say. Um it's some sensitive stuff WE accidentally found.On an island we stopped off at to get some fresh water and fruit.

ARLINGTON pours more beers. JEAN LUC is increasingly worried.

> ARLINGTON
>
> So is that where you got the money you had last night? From WILLIAM?

PAT'S drinking at an impressive clip but JEAN LUC raises his hand to slow him down. ARLINGTON reprimands JEAN LUC with a look.

> PAT
>
> It was the reward they gave us. It could have been much more though if we'd gone to a TV Network!

The other three listen intently now

> ARLINGTON
>
> I too can pay exceptionally well for unique valuable information PAT.

> PAT(HE'S WIDE EYED WITH GREED)
>
> He gave us ten thousand U.S Dollars each. A TV NETWORK would have paid us at least a hundred thousand. More!

JEAN LUC puts his hand to his forehead.

> PAT THE KIWI
>
> I could tell you everything for ..

> ARLINGTON
>
> If it's what you suggest it's worth I'll give you one hundred thousand U.S. So WHAT exactly DID you find?

PAT'S excited beyond his wildest dreams.

> CLAUDE
>
> Or maybe who?

PAT suddenly stares in surprise at CLAUDE for his guess.

PAT
We found...a BODY. Well, technically, a skeleton.

CLAUDE (A BIT DRUNK)
HAROLD HOLT or JIMMY HOFFA?

ARLINGTON grimaces at him. PAT doesn't know if CLAUDE's joking.

PAT
NO! NED BAKER. He was lost at sea with the CREW of a sloop or Ketch called BLUE SKY in late SEPTEMBER 1995 or something.

The other three are deathly silent. ARLINGTON leans forward.

ARLINGTON
You're absolutely sure of this? What else did you find?

PAT's suddenly very uncomfortable.

PAT
That's valuable information right?

He knows it is. ARLINGTON takes fifty thousand U.S dollars from his wallet and hands it to PAT.

ARLINGTON
I want to know everything before I give you the other fifty thousand.

PAT(EXCITED AND UNMINDFUL)
Well, there were some photos and letters and two old audio cassettes and um, ten undeveloped Super 8 film cartridges - apart from his skeleton.

They're all speechless. ARLINGTON looks like he might have a stroke. JEAN LUC is visibly wondering about PAT's fate.

> ARLINGTON (ICE COLD VOICE)
> And precisely where is that skeleton now?

> PAT
> They hid it somewhere on the island and took a small piece of it and some hair back for DNA testing.
> JEAN LUC
> Mon DIEU!

ARLINGTON looks furious and stunned. PAT wanders over to the Bar.

> ARLINGTON (IN FRENCH)
> C'est un catastrophe! Merde! I don't know exactly what's in that film but almost anything could be devastating for us and PELAGIC DRUMLINE. And possibly for AUGUSTIN KRANEK. Shit! Shit!

PAT returns near-legless with yet more drinks.

> MICHAEL ARLINGTON
> And this GUILLAUME-WILLIAM - he took all these things back to AUSTRALIA?

PAT nods "yes" and then nods "thanks" as ARLINGTON passes him THE other $50,000 as if it might be coming back to him shortly.

> ARLINGTON
> Do you have his contact details? Where they live or phone numbers?

PAT (AWKWARDLY)
I only know the dead guy was the fiance of the LADY who came ere. JOANNA! She had one other BLOKE with her apart from WILLIAM. Said he was BRENDAN. I heard someone say he used to be an Australian SOLDIER. The two BLOKES didn't seem to like each other. I think WILLIAM didn't trust him.

#74 EXT/INT JOANNA'S HOUSE IN TOWNSVILLE DAY

SENTINEL'S SIMON meets with JOANNA, WILL and VICTORIA.

SIMON
I'm extremely interested in the content of his film and cassettes. They might be just travel stuff..but there's a chance they might have the potential to be extremely controversial, so we need maintain high level secrecy until they're fully evaluated.

WILL
Agreed. The circumstances of his death "shouts" foul play on the high seas. This material should be taken to a safe location immediately, and then be assessed and the best edit shown on mainstream TV urgently. I have a gnawing feeling we may shortly be dealing with a highly dangerous network of lethal People. And if I'm right this house will no longer be safe house.
The others look at him in disbelief.

JOANNA
Getting a bit carried away aren't we WILL? Why-ever would you say such a paranoid thing?
He's "talking to the deaf"

and heads out into the garden

DISSOLVE TO SUNDOWN.

They now sort through the bag and record the items on a PC. NED and OTHER CREW MEMBERS HAVE RECORDED several incidents on cassette. JOANNA sorts through NED's papers and LETTERS and beams when she finds a letter NED wrote for his then unborn DAUGHTER in case he never got to see her.

VICKY is shaking as she opens the letter and gasps. For the first time since she was a LITTLE GIRL she tears up and leaves them, to read them in her room.

#76 INT. BIOKRANEK HEAD OFFICE SYDNEY AUSTRALIA.DAY. PRESENT

BUSINESS HEAVIES sit at a long table in plush OFFICES. They watch OLD FOOTAGE FROM 1995 NEWS of the NUCLEAR TEST and a NEWS-READER discusses the disappearance of BIG SKY.

#77 INT. JOANNA'S HOUSE EVENING FOLLOWING DAY.

JOANNA is still stressed but is dressed up to go out. VICKY is still in shock and worn out. JO'S grey-haired boyfriend arrives.

                    KEVIN (GRINNING)
          Hi VICKY. Maybe we'll give you a break tonight if
          your MUM will stay for breakfast pancakes..

                    JOANNA
          In your dreams ROMEO. It'll need to be a pretty
          spectacular dinner party to create that scenario.

                    VICKY
          Do you mind KEVIN! I'm about to crash anyway.
          I'm worn a frazzle.

VICKY sticks her fingers in her ears and sings loudly as they share a passionate kiss. Suddenly there's an urgent knocking at the door and JO lets WILL inside. He looks very serious.

> WILL
> I'm sorry for the spoiler alert JO but I managed to phone MAI. She thinks PAT reneged on his promise to us. If there's even a one in a hundred chance he has, you and VICKY need to go and stay somewhere else for a while: Maybe my FAMILY'S property near WAYNTON. I absolutely think we may be at risk in this location. These are absolutely not the kind of people to mess with..

JOANNA and VICKY think he's alarmist and they're upset.

> JOANNA
> This is getting out of hand WILL. We're on home soil now and no one knows our reason for being in NOUMEA. KEVIN

> JOANNA
> and I are going out to dinner and a show, but of course you're welcome to stay as long..

> WILL (SHAKING HIS HEAD)
> I know PAT dropped us in it. I can feel it! I met some of those guys. They don't take prisoners!

> JOANNA
> Well you can stay here overnight if you're worried..

He's extremely uneasy. VICKY also nods that he's welcome but They seem to have a frosty awkward relationship

WILLIAM (SHAKING HIS HEAD)
I'll stay tonight. AND Leave in the morning.
I really hope you'll change your minds by then.
Have a good night

VICKY watches them follow the path through the overgrown tropical garden and disappear and then joins WILL watching TV.

#78 EXT.JOANNA'S HOUSE. NIGHT

The couple get into KERRY's car and slowly drive up the tree-lined street. Further up is a parked and empty black MERCEDES. They pass it and drive out of view. When they're gone three hiding FIGURES appear in the car and study the house.

INT. JOANNA'S HOUSE.NIGHT.
                    VICKY
        Were you and...DAD close as BROTHERS UNCLE
        WILL

They've clearly never had much to do with each other for one reason or another and he's slightly awkward with her.

                    WILL
        We absolutely were VICKY. He was the brainy
        one and you've obviously inherited his as well as
        JO's smarts. He was two years older, and there
        wasn't much he wasn't good at. I was the rat-bag
        troublemaker of the family. But I can tell

                    WILL
        you one thing: he would have really loved you and
        been very proud of you.

It's like it's the first proper conversation they've had and VICKY is surprised as she warms to his self-deprecating manner.

VICKY

How come you never visited MUM and me? Didn't you two get on?

WILL (LONG PAUSE)

I didn't really know how to handle his death, VICKY. I was in the ARMY until you turned 19 or so. Also I was overseas for a lot of that time as well, or in PERTH. I saw a hell of a lot of stinking things PEOPLE did to each other then. Eventually I lost my ability to relate to people properly. Your MUM was messed up by it as well, so it was easier for us not to see each other. I REALLY wanted to be in your life but assumed your MUM wouldn't want that. Maybe I thought she saw me as a potential Bad influence..

VICKY

I think you're way wrong about that. Good-night UNCLE WILL.

They both grin having made a start at something. She leaves him in the lounge with the TV the only light and pats a very old dog lying in a basket in the kitchen. She switches off all other lights as she heads down the hallway to her bedroom.

#79 INT.VICKY'S BED-ROOM.NIGHT

VICKY's in shorty pyjamas in a twinkling and asleep almost the moment her head hits the pillow.

#80 EXT/INT SUBURBAN STREET AND PARKED MERCEDES. NIGHT

The three obscured FIGURES in the dark of the car watch the house for an hour. But there's no sign of anyone and no lights. Silently they exit the car and move up the street keeping to the lush tropical trees, ferns and palms that fringe the road. The three MEN split up when they reach JOANNA's garden and while two move to opposite ends of the darkened house the third moves to the veranda and the front door. Occasional flashes of lightning in the sky show their positions momentarily. WILL who's fallen asleep watching TV with the sound off is alert to the smallest noise and switches off the TV and peers through a curtain.

JOANNA'S old dog growls timidly when he hears a noise. He looks up as he sees a HUMAN SHADOW pass by the lounge-room window but is too frightened to do anything but hide. WILL rummages through his backpack silently while watching the front door. He finds a leather bag within it and removes two "loaded" hypodermic needles and a hunting knife and hurries to VICKY's room.

#81 INT.VICKY'S ROOM. NIGHT

He wakes her with a hand over her mouth and through her curtains shows her one of the attackers prowling the back garden.

> WILL
> Put on your running shoes. Hide in the ENSUITE with your Mobile on vibrate. If you hear me yell "NED"loudly, run as fast as you can out the front door and stay off the roads. Don't stop unless you hear a car and if you do, hide in the nearest dense garden at least a half mile from here. If I can end them I'll come for you.

SHE'S terrified and he gives her a hug and moves fast up the hallway despite his injury. He hides in a wall recess as the first PROWLER picks the lock and enters the house.

Heavy rain masks the sounds of the HOUSEBREAKER and another, who follows him in.

#82 INT. VICKY'S ROOM. NIGHT

The wind and rain blow through VICKY's security window-grill. She's cowering in her en-suite clutching a softball bat.

#83 INT.JOANNA'S HOUSE. HALLWAY AND LOUNGE AREA.

The MEN check out the rooms as though there's no one there. WILL ambushes one in the hallway and renders him unconscious with a punch to the back of the ear. The second he stabs with the hypodermic and the MAN falls unconscious instantly.

#84 INT. VICKY'S BEDROOM. NIGHT

He collects VICKY and they make their way to the open front door. She hides behind the lounge and WILL limps as fast as he can into the garden.

TRACKING; WILL blends with the darkness and stalks the solid figure in the garden and stabs him with the other hypodermic.

#85 INT.NED'S HIRE CAR.BRISBANE.NIGHT

VICKY's in shock but she's tough and calls JOANNA. WILL calls the Police.

> VICKY
> MUM, where are you? You can't go home tonight!

> JOANNA'S VOICE
> We're just leaving the restaurant! Whatever's happened VICKY?

> VICKY
> UNCLE WILL was right. We've just been attacked in our own home MUM. Oh MUM, They might have killed us! Thank GOD that WILL was there

JOANNA fights to breathe and her voice won't come.

#86 EXT/INT.KEVIN'S APARTMENT BUILDING.GATED-COMMUNITY.NIGHT

JOANNA AND KEVIN open the door to VICKY and WILL. JOANNA embraces her DAUGHTER.

> JOANNA DANIELS
> Who were they WILL? How did you know we could be in danger so soon?

> WILL
> No one should try to second guess people like this

#87 INT.JOANNA'S HOUSE. DAY

Two POLICEMEN interview JOANNA, VICKY and WILL. OTHER POLICE comb the GARDENS and three others dust for finger prints. ONE SENIOR OFFICER is in animated conversation on her Mobile.

#88 INT.SENTINEL HEAD OFFICE COOLANGATTA.DAY

> SIMON
> I'm really shocked by this! I've been naive and jeopardized VICKY's life. And ashamed for not conceding the extensive wider impact of this FILM FOOTAGE. We need to edit that film with JOANNA and MERYL, our Award Winning FILM and DIGITAL EDITOR and make multiple copies urgently. From this point on we need absolute secrecy. The DNA testing on the bone will be completed tomorrow and I'm bringing in some of our best SECURITY PEOPLE immediately. We can surveille JOANNA's home for a fortnight and check for other bugs.
> VICKY and anyone else who wishes can stay in one of our safe houses in BYRON BAY or CURRUMBIN.

WILLIAM
I should've been adamant last night... Look, JOANNA and VICKY should come and stay at LONE PINE with me and her GRANDPARENTS: be good for everyone

JOANNA and VICKY nod gratefully.
JOANNA
VICKY should go but I'm needed for the Edit at the Studios in BYRON BAY

WILL
Might be safer to do it at Lone Pine because those bastards might be anticipating that. You'll need more than that BRENDAN guy that's for sure, as I don't trust him. I'd like to send two of my old SAS mates for a month as extra insurance

JOANNA (GRATEFULLY NODDING)
That's a perfect solution right now. VICKY, you might like to read this other letter from your Dad I found. It's a letter to his unborn daughter.

VICKY's someone who rarely shows her emotions but she flushes and pockets it in her jacket. WILL too shows emotion

#88B INT. EDITING SUITE. SENTINEL HOUSE BYRON BAY. DAY
They're screening short edits of SUPER 8

SIMON
This first cut is mind-boggling stuff JOANNA. You'd think it was HOLLYWOOD SCHLOCK if you didn't know what we're watching was a recorded documentary footage. No wonder those evil BASTARDS wanted it at all costs.

JOANNA's too upset to speak when she sees the BIG SKY blown up

> JOANNA
> Those vile .. They deserve to ...they deserve
> summary justice.

She turns her face away from the scene shaking her head.

#89 INT WILL'S PICK-UP TRUCK. ROAD TO WAYNTON. DAY

VICKY sits next to WILL with the opened letter from NED in her shaking hands. She starts reading it to herself, but suddenly clutches the single page and looks out the window at the passing countryside. WILL knows she's weeping silently.

> WILL
> You never met your DAD, but he was a great bloke
> VICKY, and like I said, he would have been so
> proud of you.

> VICKY
> Can I read you what he wrote UNCLE WILL. He
> mentions you too.

> WILL
> I'd be honoured VICKY.

> VICKY (MORPHS INTO NED'S VOICE)
> My dearest darling DAUGHTER. Your MOTHER
> is the love of my life. And she will be the best of all
> MOTHERS to you. As you read this letter, please
> know I love you to bits just as she does though I
> now know for a terrible fact I will never meet you.
> That is unimaginably sad for me because I was
> never so excited in my life as when your MUM
> told me she was pregnant with you and I would be

> VICKY (CONT)
> a father. Even though I never held you in my arms
> or sang to you or read you to sleep, nor taught you
> to swim or took you to your first day of school, I am
> a major part of you and I pray you will sometimes
> feel my comforting presence beside you when you
> are sad or lonely or frightened. Be the best you can
> be little Sweetheart.
> When you get old enough I dearly hope you will
> go and stay with MY MOTHER and FATHER
> at LONE PINE and seek out their company and
> wisdom and also seek out the company of your
> uncle WILL, as you could not find a better FRIEND
> or FATHER figure in all the wide world. It is my
> deepest wish you both become great FRIENDS
> when I am gone.
> Remember that you are in my heart and thoughts
> for every second of what remains of my life.

WILL turns and looks out his window swallowing hard and he
pretends to adjust his dark glasses.

> WILL
> I know he would have thought all his
> CHRISTMASES would have come at once had he
> lived to see you, GIRL.

The letter has clearly done them both a power of good.

#90 INT. SENTINAL BENEFACTOR'S PRIVATE CINEMA. BYRON
BAY.NIGHT NIGHTEDITED FILMS AND FLASHBACKS TO 1995 –
NED'S PACIFIC JOURNEY

SENTINEL EXECUTIVES watch the first cut of the FILM. NED
NARRATES SOME OF THE FILM. It's scratchy in parts and bits

of the Super 8 Footage are slightly over-exposed and the sound distorted. SENTINEL FILM AND PERIODIC NARRATION

The substantial boat slices through the Pacific. NED stands on the foredeck talking to the camera while JOANNA films. People walk past in the background and when their names are mentioned they wave and say "Hello" To CAMERA. JOANNA pans to each in turn.

NED:
We left Australia on this 40 foot sloop called the BIG SKY in mid 1995 with seven crew. This is TORBEN the Danish Captain..

TORBEN:
Hello

NED:
First mate HANK

HANK:
Hello everyone

NED:
And JACKSON, OUR CANADIAN PHOTOGRAPHER:

PHOTOGRAPHER:
Hi there.

NED:
U.S SCIENTISTS LINDA and AL

CARSON:
Greetings amigos

NED:

And MARIANIQUE, a Marine Biologist: Bonjour!

The others crowd in and huddle up

ALL:
HELLOOOOO

The story is now told mostly by NED'S NARRATION on the SUPER 8 converted cassettes and we see the footage he took as amateurish Super 8 colour and sound. But The FILM IMAGERY mostly matches the Narration.

> WILL (NARRATING OVER FILM)
> We decided to take a Heading for TONGA, the COOK ISLANDS then take a new heading for PITCAIRN before turning East again. The aim was to look like island hopping YACHTIES from the U.S Or CANADA, as we were running a CANADIAN flag. The CARSON couple had already investigated testing at THREE MILE ISLAND, and at CHERNOBYL after those nuclear disasters. They were allowed limited examination the new FUKASHIMA NUCLEAR POWER PLANT site which was then being set up and they believed it would have future irreparable future problems. They were permitted limited access as well to the Australian nuclear power station at LUCAS HEIGHTS. Our sea journey was intended to gauge the wider extent of marine damage from the MUROROA and F'Angataufa ATOLL TESTS but became something much more.

The vision seen during his voice over narration is the sloop in full sail passing numerous islands and archipelagos that look like an Earthly Paradise.

> NED BAKER:
> Even now we found high level trace elements of COBALT and STRONTIUM 90 many hundreds of miles from Test areas And fish we caught and coco nut milk was dangerously irradiated.
> Unfortunately at that point JOANNA got sick and we were lucky to make NOUMEA before she really went downhill. We finally decided the

NED BAKER (CONT)

rest of us would join the protest flotilla to try to test for radioactive effluent leakage from the coral reefs and lagoons as close to MORUROA as possible, though we knew this was highly risky if we got caught. Just before our departure I learned JOANNA was pregnant with our daughter VICTORIA and I was over the moon.

We insisted JOANNA stay at the hospital NOUMEA till she recovered and then would fly home. We were concerned before we left NOUMEA when we threatened by three very aggressive MEN. One was French and another South African, but the AUSTRALIAN one reminded me of a tiger snake and warned us against sailing. I followed him later and he boarded an old MINESWEEPER. It had no markings and the name on the side was painted over but my best guess read MEPHISTO PANAMA. I could almost read an older name painted out on the side that looked like it might have been KR something. In order to carry out our intentions we hid a tiny three man submersible CYANA submarine on board in hope of testing the waters.

#91 EXT.THE BIG SKY SAILING THROUGH THE SOUTH PACIFIC. 1995

A series of DISSOLVES: They sail n a leisurely fashion towards the Test zone posing as adventure travellers.

NED (NARRATING)

There was one really harrowing incident as we made our way towards MORUROA when that same MINESWEEPER, ignoring International Law, intercepted and boarded us on the high seas. There were some eight in their CREW and a surly

NED

violent lot they were. Things were getting out of hand as they began threatening us and we sent out a MAYDAY that was thankfully answered by a small NORWEIGIAN cargo ship just as things started getting scary, as one of them actually drew a gun. The ship pulled in alongside and they had some Security PEOPLE on board and those who'd boarded us left in a hurry. But after they'd left we discovered the radio and SATNAV had been partly sabotaged. We were all very jumpy after that let me tell you

Other small vessels begin arriving outside the 15 mile French territorial zone near MORUROA atoll intending to disrupt the scheduled Test on the following day. There is also a News CREW from New Zealand in attendance to report the looming confrontation between a FRIGATE and a PATROL BOAT from the French Navy and the protest boats..

#92 EXT. ORIGINAL GRAINY NEWS FOOTAGE MORUROA. DAY

NED

On the day of the first TEST BIG SKY stayed well away from the confrontation and French fighter jets buzzed the small flotilla dangerously, Frigate moved in with force when the protesters refused to disperse and they turned water cannons on the small flotilla, stormed the boats with speed boats full of commandos and made multiple arrests.

#93 INT/EXT CYANA UNDERWATER MORUROA. DAY

AL CARTER and MARIANIQUE are in the CYANA and travel underwater into a lagoon without detection. AL steers the tiny sub along the underwater lagoon wall and studies a screen relaying what the outside camera sees. The water is dark deep down and they strafe the walls with a small bright light as a French PATROL BOAT roars across the waters far above.

> AL
>
> 200 hundred metres and steady. My calculations place one of the early detonation chambers in this area.

> MARIONIQUE (SHOCKED)
>
> There's some interference on Camera 2 These radioactive readings are off the charts. I can see stress fractures in the cliff faces but I had anticipated that.
> Caesium 134 and PLUTONIUM readings this high can only indicate one thing...

#94 EXT.UNDERWATER AT THE ATOLL. AFTERNOON

A distant POV of the CYANA makes it look extremely vulnerable.

#95 INT. CYANA. DAY

THEY'RE totally shocked to see great CRACKS in the CORAL and basalt wall and massive amounts of NUCLEAR DETRITUS and effluent streaming like a small fast flowing rivers from fissures in the cliffs.AL takes samples and films the streaming waste and immediately heads for deeper waters. His watching wife holds an instrument recording the radio-active elements and it goes haywire.

> AL
>
> The cameras got all of this, right? Then let's get the hell out of here.
> As they travel along the out reef cliff face they witness an enormous gash along the side of the cliff and another river streams from here through GEOTHERMAL PATHWAYS.

#96 EXT.BIG SKY.LOOMING NIGHT

The CREW are anxiously peering over the side of the KETCH waiting for a sign of the CYANA. Suddenly it comes to the surface and the crew help the TWO SUB MARINERS "back on board.

> AL
> The atoll will definitely cause a submarine landslide and in all likelihood something far, far worse: Guaranteed! Sink the CYANA. We need to hightail it for PORT VILA.

#97 EXT. PACIFIC.NIGHT

As the rain starts to fall they motor South at full speed. While it's a miserable night, they're all glad to be heading for VILA. NED is first watch.

#98 EXT. PACIFIC OCEAN HEADING FOR PORT VILA. DAY

The weather's foul the next day as well though strong winds pull the vessel along at a good pace. From NED'S POV the sky's in turmoil and the waves are growing.

#99 EXT.BIG SKY. NIGHT.

NED'S in the tiny crows-nest with night binoculars. He's exhausted and almost asleep on his dangerous perch. The weather is worsening as he PANS with his binoculars. He suddenly jolts in response to something he thinks he sees and jerks the binoculars back. There's a brief flash light as he discerns the shape of a DARK VESSEL pursuing them.
He almost shimmies down the steep mast and onto the deck.

#100 INT.MAIN CABIN.NIGHT

Three of the crew are sleeping and the others read or trivial Pursuit (visual dramatic irony).

NED

Listen up! I think we're being followed. I thought
I saw something an hour ago but just now I know
I did. It's maybe ten miles back. I think we need to
take extraordinary evasive action.

They all hurry on deck now in response. There's two other sets of
infra red binoculars that TORBEN and HANK now use and they
also spot it. The rest of the crew are terrified.

TORBEN

Obviously it's those same bastards that boarded us
and damaged the radio They're coming after us for
sure to..

MARIONIQUE

What for? You can't mean..?

TORBEN, HANK and NED all give her the same deadly serious
look.

JACKSON

KOREAN and JAPANESE trawlers fish these areas
don't they? Isn't there a slim chance...

TORBEN gives him a fatalistic head shake.

JACKSON

CHRIST ALMIGHTY! I never signed on to be
killed.

NED

And you think we did? It is that MINESWEEPER,
MEPHISTO. I guessed they were Mercenaries or
Pirates. Speaking of which, I'm pretty sure they
had a 20 millimetre gun on the foredeck under
canvas cover.

AL CARTER

What the hell are we going to do TORBEN?

HANK trains his binoculars into the darkness again as the moon shows between clouds.

> HANK
> NED's right. I thought I saw a mounted hidden gun. I didn't want to scare..

> LINDA CARTER (TOTALLY SHOCKED)
> You're all actually saying they're planning to kill us on the open seas?

> NED
> Yes. Sink us on the open seas with ALL HANDS on deck the way those SPIES ALAIN MAFART and DOMINIQUE PRIEUX and
> their CRONIES originally intended to do to the RAINBOW WARRIOR boat.

> LINDA (SHAKING IN TERROR)
> I can't believe how casual you are! My GOD! Isn't there something we can do?

> TORBEN
> They are gaining steadily. We have...what, one gun..

> HANK
> Two old 303's and a decent Zodiac inflatable dinghy..with a small outboard

NED, TORBEN and HANK all look at each other simultaneously with the only possible solution. The others shrug and look numb.

> TORBEN
> That weapon could sink us from half a mile at least. But there are hundreds of islands in this archipelago
> We can't outrun them, but we might just lose them. In the worst case scenario we could..

> NED (ANTICIPATING HIM)
>
> ..abandon ship in a relatively safe place and make for an island in the second dinghy and hide out.. before they blow up the ship.
> It would have to be totally dark so they don't see us escape. And we leave one dinghy on board.

TORBEN and HANK nod agreement. It was their thought too

> TORBEN
>
> There's nothing else for it then. Let's prepare.

> TORBEN
>
> NED you stock the waterproof backpack.. Super 8 FILM cartridges, audio cassettes, undeveloped photos and floppy discs Stock water, knives, an opener and as many tins of food as you can fit and carry comfortably. LINDA and AL .. flares, dry clothes and more food. HANK get the guns and ammunition

MARIONIQUE prepares the ZODIAK and with NED's help attaches it to the stern.

> TORBEN
>
> Getting into the inflatable at full speed, will be dangerous.
> DISSOLVE TO:

#101 EXT. THE OPEN SEA.NIGHT

NED stands at the stern and sights the PREDATOR SHIP. It's made up five miles and still tracks them. He glances at scattered football field-sized ISLANDS they're passing that march off towards some larger ones and the channels that link them.

#102 EXT. ISLAND CHAIN SOUTH PACIFIC NIGHT.

NED's watch shows just after midnight as the SLOOP yaws 100 metres off the sixth and biggest island of this group and sweeps into a deeper avenue of water heading across a huge five mile channel towards the stretching ARCHIPELAGO. The others stand around the bow now, leaning over the gunnel, while TORBEN remains vigilantly framed in the wheelhouse. NED climbs down into the Zodiak with some difficulty. They start handing down the packs.

          HANK
NED'll help everyone down one by one.
          JACKSON
This RIFLE cover doesn't look very waterproof but I'll take it!
HE lifts the 303 and smooths his fingers along the muzzle.
I haven't used one of these since I was a teenager in the Rockies only ever shot cans and trees though

          LINDA
If NED's plan works, we shouldn't need the guns or the waterproofing.

The Big Sky is soon cutting across a small bay. Bad light shows an island with steep-jungle-covered hills. They all fall silent at the sounds of distant engines, all the more malign for the blackness that engulfs its source.

TRACKING The BIG SKY breezes around a narrow promontory and they're in a wide bay broken by clusters of small islands. They make good time across the reaches of the BAY.

Through binoculars NED watches the sludge grey MINESWEEPER slinking past the HEADLAND; it resembles some flat occult metallic BEAST, tracking them - picking up their electronic scent; like a grey ghost steadily gaining on the smaller sloop.

> TORBEN
> If we can navigate this narrow trench… maybe they won't be able to follow

They're safely through and spirits rise a little but somehow the MINESWEEPER passes through too.

DISSOLVE TO:

THEY find THEMSELVES in yet another sombre bay, but this time huge and rimmed by a vast circlet of mountainous land.

> JACKSON
> There's another outlet to the sea by the looks of it Torben …

> NED
> It's time!

TORBEN sets the steering on automatic pilot and they all hurry to the stern.

#103 EXT. NIGHT AND DINGHY. NIGHT

It's a difficult manoeuvre under these conditions, as although the rubber craft is attached, they're moving at nine or more knots and one mistake could mean catastrophe.

TORBEN skins his hand lowering MARIONIQUE down towards NED'S waiting arms and swears as he leaps down after her. The last two are MARIONIQUE and HANK. HANK lowers her down but the attachment rope breaks and the DINGHY drifts. They can't catch the sloop, without starting the motor so HANK dives in and swims after them as they row towards him, but he's eighty metres away and starts to panic. He suddenly goes under and isn't seen again.

TORBEN
HANK! HANK?

NED (WEARING NIGHT GLASSES)
He went under. He's not coming up

They're all devastated but row for their lives regardless.

#104 EXT.DINGHY NEAR PACIFIC ISLANDS. NIGHT

Four paddles slice through the low swells as they strike out towards a sliver of beach surmounted by a JUNGLE ESCARPMENT

The muted tattoo of wood hitting water and the fading thrum of the ENGINES of BIG SKY are briefly the only noises in the cavernous lagoon. No one speaks. They hardly dare breathe. At fifty metres from the beach the MEPHISTO'S ENGINES grow loud and they stroke with absolute urgency.

NED trains the binoculars back and suddenly sees grey nose of the MEPHISTO edge into view.

NED (HARSH WHISPER)
Everyone stop rowing. Lie flat and pray they don't
see us now!"

The DINGHY drifts the last metres onto the merest dusting of volcanic sand. Noises are all around them now. Jungle rustlings in the island steeps above them, strange bird callings and the passing rumbling thunder of the warship fill the air.

TORBEN
Stay low and hide in the nearest Patch of rainforest
higher up the slope. Silently! Now!

They crawl out of the DINGHY on their stomachs hauling the dinghy after them and into the bushes.

TORBEN
Fast as you can go …now,on stomachs and knees.
No one stand, and no noise.

They struggle up the moist grassy embankment and look down
on NED as he brushes a frond along the sand where they landed.
DISSOLVE TO

Shortly they're struggling laboriously up the verdant slope clinging
to low branches of Hibiscus trees and ferns for leverage and to keep
them upright against the abruptness of the gradient. At a hundred
metres up they pause in exhaustion blowing heavily as they turn
to stare through narrow slits in the canopy down and across the
lagoon. All around them the jungle is suddenly alive with bird song
and the ructions of nocturnal animals.

MARIONIQUE
There! There look! I can see it. Sorry take these,"

She pushes the binoculars towards TORBEN's hands.

E.L.S In the eye of the lagoon TORBEN sees the closeness of the
chase now. The throb of engines drifts across the distances as he
watches transfixed the MEPHISTO bear down on the smaller sloop.
NED stares through another set of binoculars

MARIONIQUE
What's happening now Torben

They all stare in the direction in which the binoculars are focussed.
Then he speaks to himself, oblivious of the others.

TORBEN
Fox at bay. Lost his earth … nowhere to run. Brave
Blue Sky fox..

They all stare at him in awe as he mumbles to himself. can't turn

with no captain..Then the heavens
burst as a shell obliterates the Big Sky.

> TORBEN
> FUCKERS! Bloody FUCKING TURDS!

CLOSE on TORBEN'S disbelieving face as the LITTLE MERMAID
FIGUREHEAD figure-head disappears from view with all but a few
pieces of driftwood remaining.

In the storm of destruction the jungle noises that had abated now
once more they hold sway. TORBEN's inconsolable. NED takes the
binoculars and watches as the Minesweeper moves in slow circles
in the epicentre of the lagoon and huge search lights swing wide
beams of stark yellow light across the water.

Indistinguishable debris floats on the water and some of the beams
pause on patches of water for a minute or so while the ship continues
its grizzly search.

> NED
> Come on: we can't stay here TORBEN!

NED takes his arm and the DANE looks blankly at him, it now
being light enough to discern his features reasonably

> NED BAKER
> We've got to at least get to the top of this first ridge
> before daylight

Faces stare up blankly at the slope that climbs another 100 metres
to disappear in low cloud. Then they set off.

#104B EXT ISLAND SLOPE AND JUNGLE. DAY
 They struggle through the dense undergrowth. Every so often
they stop, panting, and sit uncomfortably on small plants or any
available space to regain their breath.

                    HANK
Five minutes only! We must put as much distance
between that ship and us as possible.
He sits on his hams cracking his knuckles as
he speaks. All their eyes are red-rimmed and
bloodshot.

                    MARIONIQUE
But - they have sunk the boat? They will sail soon
when they see no survivors..yes?"

                    NED
TORBEN's just saying we can't be too careful. They
just might dive..to check for bodies. Depends how
deep it is. I'm guessing really deep.

#105 EXT.MEPHISTO MINESWEEPER.DAWN

On the ship in the lagoon stark faces scan the lightening water and
the track of the searchlight. A small launch slips about the waters
hauling on board slabs and slivers of floating wreckage.

A COMMANDO standing at the front of the launch stabs his
thumb at the water.

                    LE ROI
Ca fait au fond de la piscine...Gone to the bottom
of the pool"

#106 EXT.PACIFIC ISLAND.EARLY MORNING

ON the other side of the ISLAND the dispossessed CREW lie about
breathlessly in a small clearing as the morning sun warms them.

                    NED (CASSETTE NARRATION) (CONT'D)
Some men from that MINESWEEPER dived for
the bodies but it was too deep and they sailed
away. The first island we rowed to was a poor

NED (CASSETTE NARRATION) (CONT'D)
choice as there was no food. After two days the
weather was better and we rowed the dinghy at
night for about three miles and came to a much a
more promising island. Apart from a central rise
and a few low cliffs and a small headland blocking
a view to the other side of the island it looked to
be the right choice.

#107 EXT/INT.SECOND ISLAND.DAWN

They find a cave and are able to light a fire dry their clothes.

NED BAKER (narrating)
We rested up for a single day then set out to scout
for food. On that day the very last of our luck in
this life, ran out. I had decided I couldn't eat any
more baked beans and said I was going hunting
fresh food and asked if a anyone wanted to join
me.

TORBEN and MARIONIQUE came with me but were clearly
more interested in a QUICKIE than FINDING food. They took a
knife attached to a wooden shaft, and a sack, and we explored the
shoreline.

#107B EXT. NARROW BEACH BRACKETED BETWEEN SMALL
CLIFFS AND JUNGLE.

They find a colony of big OYSTERS and spear some decent sized
crabs on a rock shelf exposed at low tide. They find some windfall
coconuts among a stand of palm trees and some yams as well.

MARIONIQUE
Um, we're going to spend some time alone. We
will meet you back at the CAVE in a few hours.
Okay.

They part at what appears to be one of several pig runs among the undergrowth. DISSOLVE TO:

#108 EXT.ISLAND JUNGLE AND UNDERGROWTH. DAY

Later NED'S bag is full of live crabs and oysters, yams and fruit and coconuts. He starts heading back to the CAVE and cuts through a patch of denser jungle in front of him. HIS way is partly blocked by a ten metre high basalt TOR in front of him. It has a forbidding look about it and in a kind of mesmerized state he drops his bag and climbs despite the steepness of the ROCK.

When he reaches the top he scans a small telescope in a wide symmetrical sweep of several compact beaches cut off from each other by falls of sizable volcanic rocks. But he stops suddenly and does a double take and directs the telescope at the TINY BAY: There moored in deeper water is their NEMESIS: the MEPHISTO. In total shock he watches several MEN working on the deck and others collecting along the foreshore. Two are drinking beers under a palm tree.
NED suddenly ducks down and lies on his back looking up at the sky in bewilderment.

From an overhead POV he takes a deep breath and slides recklessly down the steep side of the TOR, landing in dense grass. He immediately races for the fork in the jungle where he and the others went their separate ways.

He hears thrashing and in sudden fear pulls out a lethal-looking hunting knife, but is relieved to see a small WILD PIG. He follows the track at a fast pace but trips on a tree root and lies winded for a moment. On his hands and knees he suddenly hears FOREIGN VOICES growing louder. He's well hidden and can sees HERVE who threatened him and JOANNA in New Caledonia, and a much bigger swarthy-faced bald MAN.

> BALDIE(FRENCH WITH
> SUBTITLES&ENGLISH)
> I vote the beach and then some wild pig and some
> CARLSBURG beers

NED'S stunned and fearful but then visibly enraged as he visibly reflects on what their crimes. He watches them as they emerge from some dark canopy and veer off towards one of the beaches. NED follows silently and passes through a narrow defile onto a strange almost-dreamlike beach.

#109 EXT. EDGE OF LITTORAL FOREST AND ISLAND BEACH. DAY

NED creeps stealthily to the edge of a small cliff that rises from the shallows of the lapping water.

FROM NED'S POV the men have entered the water and are swimming in a leisurely fashion towards a sandbar fifty metres from the beach. CUT TO:

NED spots their CLOTHES lying near a stand of NIPA PALMS near to water's edge. He stands undecided and then runs low and dives into the long grass growing almost up to the water.
FROM NED'S LOW POV looking through grass, he sees the MEN have reached the sand bar and are taking the afternoon sun.

MOVING: NED makes a rapid sortie to their clothes. He finds a knife and a gun.

PAN TO: It's an hour later as the SWIMMERS head back to the beach. They're yelling and laughing. NED sees them in the shallows, walking onto the sand. The two MERCENARIES start drying themselves but suddenly the bigger one, looks up at the opposite end of the beach. His initial look of amazement is replaced with a delighted leering grin. NED'S face shows dismay.

#110 EXT.FULL BEACH.DAY

From his POV TORBEN and MARIONIQUE, both semi-naked, stroll onto the beach. NED's face sags.
MARIONIQUE screams and runs. TORBEN stays still in indecision. HERVE, the wiry and smaller of the two draws a knife from his belted swimming trunks and races towards TORBEN, who picks up a rock and bravely assumes a fighting posture.

CUT TO:

When HERVE is within five metres of him and running fast TORBEN throws the rock with deadly accuracy and stuns him. TORBEN immediately attacks and they fight rolling in the sand and punching and chopping at each other's throat and face.

NED watches the bigger man rummaging through his clothes and then standing with a puzzled look on his face when he realizes his gun is missing. He's found another knife though. PAN TO: FROM his POV NED now emerges from the shadows, holding the handgun concealed in a wind cheater. His face is deadly cold.

> BALDIE
>
> You! I'll kill you slow. I promise you that! And when HERVE has slit your friend's throat we will have some fun with that girl.

> NED
>
> The only thing you'll be doing for these last seconds of your life is wondering why your chest's leaking buckets of blood and why you can't breathe, you purulent scrotum

NED glances over his shoulder and sees TORBEN get his hand on HERVE'S throat and pull him helplessly down to the sand

THE DARK MAN suddenly hurls the dagger at NED just as he ducks and part of it comes out the back of his shoulder. He groans in agony as the MAN rushes towards him but NED manages to shoot his attacker so a huge dark red flower seems to be growing from his chest. NED staggers towards him and kicks him over to make sure he's dead, But NED is also in a very bad way. TORBEN suddenly arrives, with HERVE lying dead in the background.

> TORBEN
>
> Hang in there man. I will help you.

NED drops to the sand and sits in shock as blood seeps from his shoulder. TORBEN removes the knife and NED briefly faints.

TORBEN finds a shirt among their gear and uses it as a tourniquet bandage on NED. He races back up the beach and drags HERVE into deeper water and weighs his body down with some big stones and smoothes the sand with a palm frond. He races back to NED and does the same with the big man's corpse as NED wakes.

> NED
> What's happened..? I can't.

> TORBEN
> They're both dead. We killed those WEASELS. Hang in there while I .

He bandages NED's shoulder as best he can and helps him to his feet and then back to the cave.

#111 EXT/INT.ISLAND CAVE.DAY/NIGHT

All are cowering in terror when they arrive back. A tearful MARIONIQUE points the 303 towards whoever is entering the cave and then embraces TORBEN.

> MARIONIQUE
> Oh thank God..! Thank God!
> TORBEN
> Get everything. Secure the water proof bags. Test the dinghy's fully inflated. Hurry. There isn't a second to lose.

#112 EXT. DINGHY PACIFIC OCEAN. NIGHT

It's a moonless night and TORBEN, all except NED row as hard as they're able. NED drifts in and out of consciousness but at least they've been able to staunch his wound and cover it with a tight waterproof bandage. AFTER they have travelled several miles a roaring wind comes up and they risk the outboard motor that gets them another ten miles until they run out of fuel.

A series of DISSOLVES show them alternately rowing and resting until finally they are all seen slumped in exhaustion and rifting helplessly. MARIONIQUE cradles NED's head and hugs him to keep him warm. He's in a bad way.

#113 EXT/INT DINGHY . EARLY MORNING

Morning finds them drifting and enveloped by thick summer mist and fog, though all still sleep in exhaustion. Suddenly NED awakes and calls out to the others.

NED
Wake up. Listen!

The others are shivering but suddenly alert. They stare at him and listen. MARIONIQUE places her hand in the water.

MARIONIQUE
There's something out there. A Big boat, I think.

They're all totally quiet listening and hoping she's wrong.

TORBEN:
JUDAS PRIEST.

They peer into the mist in apprehension and uncertainty.

TORBEN
It might not be them. Maybe I should call out...

Suddenly the bows of a big vessel loom out of the mist coming directly for them

NED
Jump for your lives!

The vessel is so big it drives straight over them killing all except MARIONIQUE and NED instantly. They dive deep and avoid the bottom of the hull but they struggle to reach the surface again.

#114 EXT.UNDERWATER PACIFIC. EARLY MORNING

NED fights to swim up but starts to fail until MARIONIQUE drags him up with her and they broach the surface, utterly exhausted. She recovers a single life vest from the dinghy and gets the semi conscious NED into it as well as attaching the water proof pack to his back. They slowly move through the water but after a time MARIONIQUE succumbs to pain and exhaustion and slips away from him and drowns. When the sun comes up in earnest he has somehow made another tiny island beach. He drags himself to his knees and then to his feet and steps along at a tortoise pace until he finds some fresh water, which he drinks.

It starts to rain and he is fortunate enough to shelter behind some trees and where he finds a concealed cave. He struggles in and lives for long enough to write one last letter

NED (HIS HANDWRITING IS VERY SHAKY)
Dearest JOANNA. The ABSOLUTE worst has happened. They sunk our ship and tried to kill us all.
We survived for some days and fought valiantly, but tell WILL I used up my ninth life yesterday and I will soon be no more. Have a wonderful life my LOVE and never stop telling our darling little VICKY how much I love her and would have loved her forever. I miss you more than life itself BUT I'm utterly Done. It's not... so bad, to die, I'm just more fatigued than I've ever been. I doubt if I'll wake up again tomorrow but at this point in life, there's no more I can physically do. Am so

tired even trying to write.. have to sleep. Goodbye
my BELOVED..

#115 PRIVATE CINEMA BYRON BAY NOW. DAY

The SENTINEL film finished and the lights come on. The twenty or
so environmentalists and others sit in stunned disbelief and silence.
Even WILL's two S.A.S mates shake their heads in astonishment.

#116 EXT/INT. WAYNTON TOWN HALL COUNCIL AND OPEN
TOWN MEETING. NIGHT

WILL arrives with VICKY on the back of his trail bike. They
have become close - almost like a FATHER and DAUGHTER
relationship and that's good for both of them. WILL parks the bike
and VICKY finds a seat inside WAYNTON TOWN HALL. WILL
patrols around the back seemingly out of habit. Or instinct! It's a
transparent full town meeting and all the LOCALS are there. There's
Local Government REPRESENTATIVES and the crooked Council.
There's also FARMERS, MINERS, LABOURERS, TEACHERS,
STUDENTS, and a cross section of the town's workers and a
regional TV STATION's CREW. And also, some harrassed-looking
CITY BUSINESSMEN.

The MAYOR looks threatened as the COUNCILLORS clearly did
not expect the Media or such a public response: They're apprehensive

>   MAYOR BRIAN BROADBENT
>   Good evening LADIES and GENTLEMEN
>   ..WELCOME to this open extra-ordinary
>   meeting of the WAYNTON TOWN LOCAL
>   COUNCIL for RESIDENTS and INTERESTED
>   PARTIES. You'll know from our local Editor and
>   JOURNALIST AARON GABLE and from the
>   SHIRE'S's FAIRFAX TELEVISION STATION,
>   we are facing a momentous time in the history of
>   WAYNTON and we are at the crossroads of a level

of unprecedented potential growth and prosperity if we only have the good sense to seize the day.

> VOICE 1 (FROM CROWD)
> Greed's BENT 'nd BROAD IN this COUNCIL!

There's laughter at this and sporadic clapping.

> MAYOR BROADBENT (ANGRY)
> This meeting won't proceed if there're more interjections and proper rules of decorum prevail; COUNCILLOR GAME will accept and review any other questions for their acceptability. Now.. back to where I was interrupted. We the people of WAYNTON have a number of exceeding wealthy overseas companies showing immense interest in the location, and its location and mineral resources, especially coal, and it also appears this wonderful shire of ours is blessed with major reserves of coal seam gas resources ....

> A VOICE from among the packed standing audience at the back
> VOICE
> FRUCK, FRACKING! To hell with C.S.G!
> And to Hell with this bent COUNCIL, you sell outs!
> The people of RAINFOREST VALLEY don't want a bar of it and nor do any real AUSTRALIANS. Remember GEORGE BENDER

There are some ROWDIES who cheer the outspoken VOICE. But there also seem to be some PEOPLE there who are looking for a big sale though they're reluctant to show it.

A group of THREE TOUGHS sitting near the back start to mingle among the more vocal parts of the crowd to target the troublemaker and any other would be-troublemakers. A close view of two of them reveal HEINZ and JAPIE, two MERCENARIES from the attempted murder of FELITI in the early scene.

WILL is in the standing crowd. He studiously watches these PROFESSIONALS doing "crowd control". He's an expert and moves among the crowd in close proximity to the three.

> INTERJECTOR (YELLING)
> Remember what happened to GEORGE BENDER!
> Remember DARLING DOWNS. End the bloody
> MINING ACT. Get a ROYAL COMMISSION. We
> ALL have to fight this

Many voices rise in unison.

> NUMEROUS VOICES:
> Remember GEORGE BENDER. NO MORE
> FRACKING.

JAPIE homes in on the Interjector, who's near the door, and manoeuvres him outside so quickly and efficiently no one notices: No one except for WILL.

JAPIE holds the TEENAGER in an arm lock and frog marches him around a laneway out of sight

> ANDREW (TEENAGER)
> You're really hurting me let me go…I haven't done
> anything..

> JAPIE
> Yes you have BOY. You've got a fucking smart
> MOUTH on you and now it's gotten you into
> trouble hasn't it? This a free lesson in etiquette
> BOY: While it will hurt, it will also be a free
> important lesson for you.

He lifts his arm to strike but suddenly WILL's there and punches him in the kidney and then the testicle, winding him and bringing him to his knees. JAPIE's buckled over with his eyes closed and doesn't know who's beaten him.

> WILL
> If my memory serves me right, the words are
> FUTSAKE SPRINGBOK. NOBODY comes into
> OUR TOWN and bullies our local people.Nobody!
> WILL whispers to the youth
> Get straight home KID. Let me know if you see
> that guy around town again. Stay right away from
> him.

The youth pats him on the back.

> YOUTH
> Thanks a heap, WILL

The whole town seems to know WILL. He watches the kid disappear into the night.

#117 INT. TOWN HALL MEETING.NIGHT

WILL manages to get inside again with no one noticing and works his way thought the crowd to grab a spare seat when someone leaves. He keeps an eye on the other two HEAVIES. The mood is distinctly frosty inside the hall and it looks like getting out of hand, but the opposition doesn't have a good spokesperson until a woman in her mid-forties accepts her opportunity to address the huge crowd. She gets WILL's attention straight away as she's attractive, but also smart and a speaker with conviction.

> LAUREN BROWN
> Yes, I'm am an American.. and yes, I've only been
> here for one year on a Teacher exchange. But I've
> come to love this country as my own and I'm
> looking at ways to get Residency if I can.

The look on the MAYOR's face says "NO CHANCE! NEVER!

> I don't know if my being an AUSSIE by disposition and hoping to legally become one, is enough to qualify me to speak here..

A general murmur of approval encourages her.

> but I hope it does. And I'm also from a small town - in COLORADO -and I do know something about coal seam gas mining or C.S.G as the MINING MAGNATES like to call it, which is kind of a selective euphemism that makes it sound like a harmless coffee sweetener or something, rather than a legislated extraction process for poisoning people, as well as ruining good land and poisoning water..

This comment causes several raised angry voices but mostly approval and clapping and she's now got everyone's attention

> LAUREN
> I can tell you there's not much good to report about coal seam gas Mining apart from profits for a few Rich disinterested companies and people who live in rich remote houses far, far, from contaminated air and farming water and leaking methane and sick kids and ruined farmland and threats to drinking water and even dangerous seismic activity.
> A growing number of countries and U.S States are banning it completely and so should this town. The documentary film GASLAND is not promoted for mainstream viewing here or anywhere else, and with good reason. Because if you watched it and read the statistics and the damage fracking does to FARMLANDS and CHILDREN and ADULTS' health, none of YOU PEOPLE wouldn't have a bar of it.

There's a sudden outburst of applause from many of the LOCALS and consternation among the MINING TROUBLEMAKER ring-ins in the audience.

> LAUREN
> I'd hate someone from another country coming to COLORADO and telling me what's wrong with MY State or country but I only want to tell a few home truths because I think this country is Paradise on Earth and it has so much Economic potential without the MINING that's tearing up the countryside. Anyway, that's all I wanted to say right now.
> She gets a loud applause. WILL looks slightly smitten for the first time ever. Now local CHINESE AUTRALIAN Australian PHIL WONG is invited up on the stage to have his say.

> PHIL
> You all know me. I cook the best Asian food in town in my PAN ASIA Restaurant and the PUB BISTRO .. AND we've two got specials tonight in both venues and I recommend the DIM SIM and CANTONESE Fish cakes

He gets a laugh for his irreverence but it calms down the mood in the Hall: For a full minute!

> PHIL
> Yeah I may cook Asian food, but I can also cook bloody good AUSSIE food too. I was born in this Valley and it's my home and my KIDS' homeland. I'm as AUSSIE as any of you here tonight and no one can deny it. I love this country and I'm willing to fight for it! But are all of you? Because there's a battle coming and it's not in some Faraway field or

> PHIL (CONT)
> desolate Badland: It's already begun in RAINTREE VALLEY to the north and it's now come to us in RAINFOREST VALLEY. And here in WAYNTON and even in the magnificent JABINGARRA FOREST and it's designated Cultural Heritage and on the U.N List.

There's suddenly deathly quiet in the hall and all eyes are riveted on him. WILL studies the faces of the outsiders and the Mayor and his cronies who are all are seriously on edge. THE Mayor wants PHIL silenced though most there want him to talk

> PHIL
> I have to tell you all this now or I swear I'll burst. Very recently..in my own restaurant, I overheard a truly frightening conversation..

A senior Policeman starts walking up the stage steps to intervene and the Mayor looks apoplectic. Other locals stand when they see he's going to be muzzled and the mood looks dire.

> PHIL(TALKS FASTER SEEING WHAT'S AFOOT)
> Like many of you, I have noticed very senior Executives from CHINA around the town and valley lately.
> Now I've got nothing whatsoever against the CHINESE..

There's general laughter.

> INTERJECTOR
> Yeah, your DAD used to be one

PHIL

That's right! They're a great PEOPLE an important ally and a mightily talented PEOPLE. But the Executives I accidentally overheard in my Bistro Just happen to be from the massive HUAN HUA GLOBAL RESOURCES COMPANY and they've now got close links to BIOKRANEK GLOBAL and I think that company CEO is the ANTICHRIST!

The MAYOR and his cronies are stunned and stand to shut him up. The Mayor motions for the POLICE to remove him, which the crowd sees and rise angrily to shout it down.

CROWD (SHOUTING AS ONE)
LET HIM SPEAK!

PHIL

The BOOK "The Art of War" was written by a brilliant CHINESE tactician long ago but those Executives neglected to read all of it, as one of the key rules is NEVER UNDERESTIMATE YOUR ENEMY.
And those GUYS did: THOSE Companies want to buy THE FARM, THE WHOLE FARM AND NOTHING BUT THE FARM. Oh yeah, And the RIVER and the FOREST and take it over.

First WAYNTON and then bit by bit...: Mark my words. Can you imagine CHINA

PHIL

or any other frigging country allowing us to buy MINES and houses and prime land in their country and then bring in their own WORKERS? What's going ON!! How dumb are WE AUSTRALIANS! This is criminal treachery on the part of our second Eleven Governments. It betrays

PHIL (CONT)
what all our pioneers and people fought for two
hundred years. Politician Real Estate arseholes
DO NOT and NEVER have owned this country.
SOME of our POLITICIANS are no different
from THAI DRUG DEALERS selling off our kids'
futures!

The first POLICEMAN grabs his arm and starts to force him off the
stage but PHIL grabs the Mike and keeps talking then yelling

PHIL
This is our CHIDREN'S' country too and no living
AUSTRALIAN has a right to steal it from them.
Most of you haven't had to fight in a war but if
you're a TRUE PATRIOT you have to start fighting
now the way all those AUSTRALIANS before us
did – and who died for this country at MESSINES
RIDGE and at LONE PINE, and on the KAKODA
TRAIL.

There's TWO COPS now fighting him off stage and for the Mike
as he shouts and another cop grabs him and he's pulled off stage
to cheering and multiple scuffles break out aided and abetted
by the three from PELAGIC DRUMLINE and the ring-in paid
TROUBLE-MAKER MINERS. More POLICE arrive and there are
several arrests as a large aggressive senior POLICEMAN comes on
stage and addresses the crowd.

WARWICK HAWKINS
I'd like everybody to resume their seats. Right
now, or I'll be laying multiple charges.
I'm the new Police Chief in town. My name is
WARREN HAWKINS. Now know this: I will
NEVER accept this kind of behaviour in a public
place in this town, ever again. This meeting is

WARWICK HAWKINS (CONT)
postponed as of now. It will be conditionally
reconvened in two weeks' time and there will be
limited numbers permitted, the terms of which
are yet to be decided. Good night

HAWKINS
LADIES and GENTLEMEN. And I use those
words advisedly.

The people file out into the night. The mood augurs badly for the
future.

#118 INT.OCEAN RIVER PUB WAYNTON.NIGHT

Many of the LOCALS reconvene for an unofficial meeting in the
local pub as they know when they've been had.

NED and VICKY enter the pub and he sees JAPIE and his two
MATES drinking and looking very aggressive. JAPIE'S still rubbing
his kidneys and moving gingerly when he sits down. He's shaking
his head, presumably telling them he doesn't know what his
assailant looked like but WILL keeps his voice low when he talks to
locals this night. WILL's a popular bloke, not something he needs to
advertise here tonight.

VICKY'S impressed when a number of tables offer for him and
VICKY to join them but he sees LAUREN BROWN sitting in the
only quiet corner talking to an older woman readying to depart.

WILLIAM
Can you give me fifteen minutes VICKY? Be
straight back unless I get lucky. In which case I'll
call you to join us.

She doesn't realize what he's up to until She sees where he's going. She gives him the thumbs up with a grin. He times his walk perfectly and she's alone when he arrives.

> WILL
> Hello. I was impressed with what you said tonight LAUREN. Was wondering if I might buy you a drink and join you.

She gives him a curious and not uninterested look.

> LAUREN BROWN
> Thanks for the offer but I was intending to leave in ten minutes.

> WILL
> What if I can hold your interest in a conversation for more than ten minutes; would you let me buy you a drink then?

She pouts, then shrugs and gives a half smile.

> LAUREN
> You're that confident, erm?

> WILL BAKER
> WILL! As in where there's a WILL there's a way.

She proffers her hand.

> LAUREN
> I'm actually really tired as I was teaching most of the day. I tell you what though: If you can tell me a story that makes me laugh, you've got a deal on the drink.

WILL

Can't I just play some BILLY CONNELLY CD tracks?

LAUREN BROWN

No BILLY C: Just a story YOU tell me!

He pauses and "visibly racks the storehouse of his memory".

WILL

Hmmm. Okay then. My friends MARTINA and JOEL have a new house in a new suburb, and a couple of kids - FELIX, a baby boy and a cherubic little girl of four named TAMMY. Next door to them is an empty block where a team of builders have just started putting up another new house. Anyway, MARTINA does a lot of gardening in the front yard with FELIX in the pram and TAMMY playing there. TAMMY makes friends with the BUILDERS and they're a friendly bunch who take a shine to her and she to them as she's always very interested in what they're doing.

After a while they kind of adopt her for an hour or so each day and get her to help them with little jobs. They get her a toy wheelbarrow and toy bricks to deliver around the site and even a little hard hat with her name on it. Course she can't go anywhere near the real building. Anyway, after a couple of weeks they start paying her ten dollars in coins a week for the help she gives them...

MARTINA approves of this and thinks it's good for her to learn about

WILL

money, so after a few weeks they visit a branch of a Bank where MARTINA'S conservative Bank Teller friend MARY works. Pretty soon Mother and daughter are sitting in MARY's office and setting

WILL (CONT)

up a Savings account for TAMMY. MARY says "I'm very impressed with you TAMMY. Working and saving money at such a young age is an important lesson in life. So tell me, will you be working with the builders on site next week as well?" Little TAMMY's eyebrows crinkle and she answers in a tiny little girl's voice, "If those WANKERS FROM BORAL DELIVER THE FUCKING BRICKS I WILL"

WILL watches the beginning of a grin growing on LAUREN's face.

WILL BAKER

Technically, that's not a laugh. I've got plenty more though. I actually know five hilarious Political jokes. You saw most of them on stage tonight

LAUREN

Boom boom! I'll have a glass of Rose thanks WILL. MATEUS if they have it.

He goes and buys them wines and returns with an optimistic smile.

WILL

You spoke with compelling conviction tonight. I can almost guarantee you some people will be thinking you should run for you run for Council and even Mayor, in the coming elections. And I'm one of them!

She makes a face at him as if to say he's crazy.

LAUREN

Surely I'd need to be an Australian citizen to do that.

WILL shrugs

LAUREN

So, I introduced Myself in the town hall. What's your story? You don't look like the typical WAYNTONIAN.

WILL

Fifth generation born and bred. The River Ocean runs through my veins. Attended the local high school where you teach, till Matriculation year and then went to Agricultural College for the last year.

My BROTHER NED was the brains of the family. He won all the scholarships going and was a big time LAWYER. See that attractive young WOMAN over there..that's his DAUGHTER and my NIECE He waves to VICKY and she waves to them both I helped manage my Family's Farm for seven years and then "ran away" to join the Army because the Circus was full up and weren't taking on anyone else.

She looks at him more closely.

LAUREN

And what would you have done in the Circus if you'd got in.

WILL

Being fired out of a cannon was my special skill. She's pretty intuitive

LAUREN

I can see in your face you've seen dreadful things and known excessive pain. Were you ..badly injured?

He glances away for a second and takes a breath. Then he risks all as he pulls up the bottom of his trouser and shows his prosthetic leg. The risk is worth it and she looks him at him with compassion and potential.

#120 EXT. JABINGARRA FOREST. SUNSET

A couple of local indigenous TEENAGERS are riding trail bikes at the edge of the magnificent State forest. They pause astride their bikes behind a group of bunched eucalypts and watch as a mysterious enormous truck carrying a large covered machine rumbles past them with a van following full of WORKMEN. They drive past a large sign reading: JABINGARRA ABORIGINAL HERITAGE AND COMMONWEALTH GOVERNMENT FOREST.PRIVATE OR LICENSED ACCESS ONLY. The small convoy drives along an unmade road and deep into the forest. Both YOUTHS clearly think it extremely suspicious

The YOUTHS follow the trucks and cars into the Forest along a fire break trail but when it starts getting dark they can't risk turning their bike headlights on and turn back towards WAYNTON.

#121 INT.JABINGARRA HERITAGE FOREST. NIGHT

The mystery TRUCK has found a sizable forest-clearing. A dozen LABOURERS get out of the two cars and set to work.

The machines are brought down off the trucks on a kind of automated metal elevator and they're revealed as a cutting edge high tech compact Fracking and Stealth Drilling machine and it makes surprisingly negligible noise when it commences drilling.

#122 INT WAYNTON. CAFE.NEXT MORNING.

WILL and VICKY are breakfasting and looking at maps of neighbouring RAINTREE VALLEY.

VICKY

Last night really scared me WILL. It's like I woke up from a coma. The companies I work for are part of the problem and I gradually learned many of the shady and suss companies my bosses deal with are subsidiaries of BIO KRANEK. I can't pretend anymore. I couldn't help seeing the extent of their involvement in everything from armament developments with six countries, cover ups in Nuclear Power in BULGARIA, ROMANIA, Ukraine and FUKASHIMA and hiring MERCENARIES. All my work was about covering their backsides for their mistakes and dirty secrets. And one was even a cover up by the Air Force base at Williamstown NSW. It's an outrage!

WILL's convinced she's her DAD's GIRL

They're finishing breakfast when LAUREN spies them through the window and comes into join them. WILL checks his watch

WILL

Hello MISS. Aren't you supposed to be taking a year 9 ANIMALS Class around about now?

She doesn't answer for a moment and is suddenly upset

LAUREN (SHOCKED)

Guess what: I may no longer have a job! My unprincipled principal told me this morning I was being suspended because of my Public expression of divisive and unsubstantiated political statements beyond the tolerable freedom range of Exchange TEACHERS. I have to attend a full day's inquiry in front of some Ethics Board in Sydney, in two days' time.

WILL'S SPEECHLESS. VICKY SHAKES HER HAND COMICALLY

> VICKY
> Congratulations LAUREN. I too am now jobless. They sacked me once they realized my PARENTS were among their mortal enemies.

WILL'S stunned by both pieces of News.

> WILL (TO LAUREN)
> I would have thought having TEACHERS who actually stand up for genuine national values and legitimate causes they believe in would be exactly what you want in a teacher. And you VICKY…I'm impressed you're no longer with those blood suckers. Let's try to forget this for the moment. LAUREN- come with VICKY and me to RAINTREE VALLEY to Shut the Gate demonstration against that big C.G.E company trying to drill on KEN WENDERS'S property. He's been fighting that company for eight years and they'll stuff up his bore water if they drill on his land and ruin the farm's potential for growing anything but weeds.

> VICKY
> And I can help you get your job back LAUREN. I'm a pretty good Pro Bono LAWYER right now.

#122B EXT/INT. NED'S CAR ON ROAD TO RAINTREE VALLEY

It's not a long drive. There's a crowd there and they're vocal. There's also POLICE, SECURITY GUARDS out of uniform, Agents Provocateurs on both sides of the barricades.

> THREE FERAL DEMONSTRATORS
> (CHANTING)
> Lock the gates, None shall pass. C.S.G can kiss my arse.

DEMONSTRATORS
NO CSG in New South Wales! No BLACKWELL MINING AND NO KIOKRANEK!

SPOKESWOMAN
THE AUTHORITIES are lying through their teeth. COAL SEAM GAS MINING poisons the Water Table and they know it - it's Asbestosis for the Land and this C.S.G company has the same moral compass as JAMES HARDY'S HIDING FROM responsibilities over ASBESTOS related deaths among their past employees. Look at their record. Keep them out. LOCK THE GATES TO ALL POINTS GLOBAL AND BIO KRANEK!

SECURITY forces seem to be very reactive and spoiling for a fight. VICKY talks to some of the DEMONSTRATORS

VICKY
WILL, see those two macho MEN over there - I've seen them in one of the employees' "No Go" areas at ALL POINTS GLOBAL. Someone told me they did undercover work for BIOKRANEK.

WILL
I see 'em. They were "Trouble-Shooting at the Town meeting.

Some of the younger DEMONSTRATORS advance on the POLICE and SECURITY and aggressive MINER ring-ins and the SECURITY- over-react massively. There are sporadic fights and a number of the ENVIRONMENTALISTS GET ROUGHED UP. A young WOMAN'S pushed by a SECURITY MAN so VICKY decks him, which impresses WILL. But a lot of the conflict is recorded and some makes the TV News. WILL and the WOMEN return to LONE PINE.

#123 EXT. LONE PINE BARN. SATURDAY MORNING

WILL's organized a secret meeting in the LONE PINE BARN. There's about 40 of the most active LEADERS in the town there, including FARMERS and a few of his old FOOTBALL TEAM. There's LAUREN, VICKY and the Head LIBRARIAN, as well as three local ABORIGINAL ELDERS. People sit on hay bales fold up chairs they're brought or stand.

WILL starts addressing them when a very big SAMOAN is ushered in by EDITH BAKER, followed by JEAN LUC from NOUMEA.

>   EDITH
> These two nice MEN have come all the way from the NORTH to help you SON: JEAN LUC from NOUMEA and FELITI from QUEENSLAND.

WILL is bemused..

>   WILL
> JEAN LUC? Seriously? I have to say this is a shock. I never expected...

>   JEAN LUC
> MON AMI CLAUDE died of the MORUROA LEUKEMIA a week ago. I'm too old to fight but I know your excremental enemy PELAGIC DRUMLINE, and I can and want to help you.

WILL's grateful and makes him welcome

>   FELITI
> My name is FELITI VAIAA and I've come down to help you all in your fight against these Companies and especially against those MERCENARIES. There are a lot OTHERS who up there who would help as well. I've been watching the TV with your demonstrations and meetings and I recognized some very BAD MEN from NEW CALEDONIA ..working for these SCUMBAGS.

WILL knows what he's going to say AND JEAN LUC too.

> WILL
> Thanks for joining us FELITI. He speaks to FELITI aside
> You can stay at our homestead till this is over. Most welcome.
> I'll talk to you about the NEW CALEDONIA matter a bit later. We're all here today because we recognize this is no longer about getting annoyed with our enemy or writing to our REPRESENTATIVES to complain. This is now a fair-dinkum BATTLE and we need to organize properly. I am going to bring in a couple of my SOLDIER MATES from the MIDDLE EAST and we are prepared to train all those who are truly ready for action. We've only got a couple of days and there are risks Though, so leave now if you're not prepared for potential bad situations

But NO ONE does.

#124 EXT/INT. LONE PINE HOMESTEAD DAY.

Most of the crowd gone but WILL and FELITI are in deep conversation when RUSSELL the Elder and two ABORIGINAL TEENAGERS arrive on trail bikes.

WILL approaches them and although we can't hear what's said they are obviously telling WILL bout the drill in the forest and he's livid and makes some heated phone calls on his Mobile.

#125 INT.SENTINEL SAFE HOUSE AND STUDIO BYRON BAY.

JOANNA and several others are showing rushes of their new film about BIG SKY to Senior ABC people and the Editors of three Broadsheet newspapers..

> JOANNA
> This is going to cause a seismic POLITICAL wave
> felt around the world.

> SIMON
> And to complete the analogy, the fall out will be
> dire. Great work everybody. I think we can get a
> dozen public showings in the U.K, L.A and Sydney
> and Melbourne at the same time. EVERYONE
> NEEDS TO SEE THIS.

#126 EXT DAY. JABBINGARRA FOREST.DUSK

WILL, FELITI, VICKI and RUSSELL sit astride TRAIL BIKES and
glide through the dense FOREST but the bikes are too noisy so they
dismount and hide the bikes and go on foot. They're careful and
stop every now and again to listen for the machinery. WILL carries
a hand gun and VICKY carries a video recorder. RUSSELL knows
the forest well and directs them towards a place where the trees thin
out somewhat. When they hear a low drilling noise they make their
way quietly through the FOREST towards that sound.
VICKY videos them as they go.

After a hundred metres they see a clearing and several basic
aluminium demountable structures for temporary accommodation.
VICKY films this and when they see the amazing stealth drill in full
operation she films that as well. BIOKRANEK INTERNATIONAL
is printed on the side of the drill and on the truck.

> WILL
> Did you get enough evidence VICKY?

> VICKY
> It's utterly damning. KRANEK are up to their
> necks in CRAPOLA. The gob- smacking arrogance
> of it beggars belief: To drill illegally here against all
> COMMONWEALTH LAWS!
> Un-less they're friends with the some human
> excrement at the top or something.

> RUSSELL
> These bastards have just declared war on us! People will die over this and I won't be held responsible. It ends tomorrow!

He's beyond fury and WILL has to restrain him as they quickly head back for the BIKES.

#127 INT/EXT. RUNNIT ISLAND DOME. DAY

KRANEK AND TORSTEN watch KRANEK'S luxury yacht bobbing on the sea from his lofty view on top of the truly frightening RUNNIT DOME.. It's almost like he's in his element in this evil place watching the world passing and being incapable of empathy.

> KRANEK
> First time I've been outside the yacht in months. This RUNNIT DOME is amazing TORSTEN. And you say it's totally a nuclear waste dump underneath. What does our THINK TANK DIVISION say about sealing or removing it?

> TORSTEN
> Still working on it. I just pray there are no major TIDAL WAVES before we do manage to seal it properly
> The VULCANOLOGIST is arriving by helicopter in a few hours with all the results for MORUROA and FANGATAUFA. I think we need the whole team examining that data.

#128 RAINTREE VALLEY PROPERTY LOCK THE GATE DEMO. MORN

There's a big chanting crowd still there and six of the toey security GUYS are DRUMLINE. FELITI, in a hooded tracksuit wends through the crowd till he picks out JAPIE and MARC and approaches a pair of earnest young twenties DEMONSTRATORS.

> FELITI
>
> G'day you blokes. Do you wanna make
> $50 bucks each for five minutes' work?
> Of course they do
> See that humungous SKINHEAD and the younger
> BLOKE wearing flak pants and DOC MARTENS?

They do. He hands each of them a fifty and makes their day.

> FELITI (LOOKING AT HIS WATCH)
>
> It's now 9 A.M. At exactly 10.30 A.M I need you
> two to approach that pair in a friendly fashion and
> say exactly this: "An hour ago a POLYNESIAN
> GUY paid us fifty dollars each to speak to you at
> 10.30 A.M. He told us to tell you he's come to even
> the score. Said His name was FELITI and that
> he's a better SWIMMER than you DRUMLINE
> DICKHEADS thought…his words, not ors." Um..
> he swore then but I won't say what he called you
> both.
> The last thing he said was to "tell them I'll meet
> I'll meet them in the JABINGARRA FOREST at
> Midday today.

#129 EXT.ROAD NEAR RAINTREE PROPERY DEMONSTARTION

FELITI takes a last look at the confrontation and looks at the road sign. It reads WAYNTON: 150 KILOMETERS. He revs the NORTON once and heads back up the highway

#130 INT. LONE PINE OUT BUILDING NEAR JABINGARRA FOREST.MORNING

WILL, RUSSELL, FELITI and two of their toughest League MATES are in camouflage gear, holding hand guns and in serious discussion.

There's a sudden low motor sound outside and when WILL opens the barn door, five of his ex SAS MATES ride in on amazing 250 C.C STEALTH BIKES. The BIKE make bears the name BIOKRANEK. They greet WILL as family.

> WILL (TO THE LOCALS AND FELITI)
> RUSSELL, FELITI, JIM and BERT, these are my "BROTHERS" from my UNIT. Meet CURLY, LARRY, MOE, GROUCHO and HARPO, my RATBAG ARMY MATES. If we get through this you'll learn their real names over many beers. Great BIKES by the way LARRY

> LARRY
> They're world first state of the Art stealth dirt bikes: Five of a first run of five hundred and five of the five that were secretly reported stolen from KRANEK International ENGINEERING AND TECKNOLOGIE works in Frankfurt. They'll carry two PASSENGERS no worries - at speed and in silence. When do we leave?

Will's OTHER MATES distribute small automatic weapons. One has plastic explosive.

> WILLIAM
> OKAY, THE A PLAN is to damage the drill engine so it needs a total replacement, and that'll take a week. JIM will film the whole EPISODE..with selective omissions. Remember they play for keeps and those DRUMLINE lot actually will try to kill us; but we just want to disarm and capture them if possible. Being caught in the act allows no room for denials. SENTINEL and an ABC TV crew are on standby if we can do this. If it goes pear-shaped it's everyone for himself and just don't get caught. They'll make an example of us if we do and we'll

likely go to maximum security prison.
To the local MEN

> WILLIAM (CONT)
> You GUYS have been great, but we're professional and I don't want you blokes shooting anyone unless you're in fear FOR your lives. You stake the perimeter and we'll do the direct stuff. Okay. Emergency back up only. We need to debilitate all of them and the TV crew need to discover them in flagrante as it were.

They're all business and shake each other's hands before setting off.

#131 EXT. LOCK THE GATES DOMONSTRATION SITE. DAY

The young DEMONSTRATORS approach JAPIE and MARC relay FELITI'S message. They turn white as ghosts and run for their bikes and phone the others.

#132 INT.KRANEK'S YACHT.DAY HELIPAD. DAY

TORSTEN meets VULCANOLOGIST VINCENT and they head for the MEETINGS ROOM. KRANEK is furious and distressed at what he hears.

> DR VINCENT
> I know it's not what you want to hear MISTER KRANEK but I'm certain it's a not a matter of "if" but "when". I utilized several mini subs with S.O.T.A quality recording sensor cameras and they circumnavigated the atoll taking readings from all parts of the atoll. I have measured and monitored the effluent stream and the gaping cracks in the basalt casing first hand and the two smallest subs went inside some of those fissures and evidenced first-hand what this disaster is. The data they submitted before we remotely destroyed them was

frightening. I've presented all requisite data
DR VINCENT
to the super computers I.T matching projections
and the stress readings keep coming up with
the same estimates and outcomes. It IS going to
implode and it IS going to cause a tidal wave of
significant dimensions. There WILL BE deadly
quantities of plutonium, caesium 34 and cobalt 60
disseminated across thousands of miles of ocean
and the wave will inundate a vast number of low
lying island communities.
Best case scenario is a TEN METRE
RADIOACTIVE TIDAL WAVE of a calamitous
nature. Worst case scenario – it will be twenty
five metre Radioactive tidal wave . MORUROA is
not saveable with any kind of concreting or mass
boulder dumpings. I deeply regret bearing such
terrible news MISTER KRANEK..

KRANEK stares at him a long minute weighing the meaning of it.
KRANEK
Who else knows about this?

VINCENT
Well, my current Assistant and two other
Researcher. And the CHIEF SCIENTIST
D'Outremer et POLYNESIE FRANCAISE
and Senior ADMINISTRATOR of Territoires
Exterieure of course will know tomorrow when
I am to deliver a world a red light Alarm NEWS
broadcast warning for the SOUTH PACIFIC and
South East ASIA and Australasia. Many islands
will need to be evacuated immediately. Goodbye
MR KRANEK.

AUGUSTIN watches him dourly as he goes. He looks at TORSTEN

with a scrunched mouth and narrowed eyebrows as he shakes his head slowly about VINCENT. The directive is unequivocal and TORSTEN follows the DOCTOR.

#133 EXT.HELIPAD.THE LUXURY YACHT CORSAIR. DAY

> TORSTEN
> We should take the helicopter to PAPEETE with him.

> KRANEK
> I don't believe him. We sail to Tahiti TORSTEN.
> I am taking that chopper and taking a week off. I will rejoin you in Papeete

#134 EXT.JABINGARRA FOREST. DAY

WILL and the S.A.S VETS ere in full camouflage gear and are like NINJAS. RUSSELL watches in admiration as they take out nine MEN in a twinkling with TRANQUILIZER DARTS and with fists and cudgels. They destroy the DRILL's engine and use handcuffs on the workmen and the two DRUMLINE SOLDIERS. WILL checks in with the OUTLIERS on their MOBILES.

> WILL
> THE real PELAGIC DRUMLINE will reach the forest very soon. We have to stop them from reaching the DRILL site and need to set up the traps now. They'll be wary and will all be on bikes.

#135 EXT.JABINGARRA FOREST. DAY

EIGHT HEAVILY ARMED MEN on powerful dirt bikes ride into the forest. They spread out but take the main trails for safety reasons. JAPIE is on the trail WILL's chosen and he runs over some spikes WILL's hidden in ground cover. His bike punctures instantly and throws him off. JAPIE struggles to his feet but WILL appears and puts him down and out with a straight right. WILL gags him and handcuffs him to a sturdy low branch.

> WILL
> Sleep tight DOPEY: I'm going after GRUMPY and LUMPY now..

JAPIE doesn't even see him. CUT TO

Along another trail FELITI waits in ambush and spies MARC and the AUSSIE CLIVE, on bikes. They brake at the TREE BLOCKADE he's made and get off their bikes to clear it. He attacks and is merciless. He disarms them and fights BOTH at the same time but they're no match for this threshing machine. FELITI knocks MARC senseless and then goes for CLIVE, but the terrified AUSSIE is too quick and he speeds off on his bike the way he's come. But FELITI won't stop this time: It's CLIVE and JAPIE he wants most.

MOVING. THEY SPEED THROUGH THE DENSE FOREST OFTEN JUST EVADING INSTANT DEATH AND BOTH KNOW IT'S TO THE DEATH.

#136 EXT. RURAL RAINFOREST VALLEY.LATE AFTERNOON

It's a race like no other. They're very skilful RIDERS and race over wild terrain and through grazing sheep herds and a hydroponic GARDEN and out onto the BACK ROADS. They're racing parallel to the OCEAN RIVER where it's most polluted and where remnants of ugly little factories are. There's an old narrow WALKING BRIDGE three metres high they mount on the bikes. It spans the river and the two race their bikes so close and so fast it's clear one of them will go over. And one does: It's CLIVE and he's sent careering off into the middle of the river.

FELITI dismounts and is about to dive in after him when he spies ONE OF THE LOCAL BULL SHARKS. And so does CLIVE and he screams for help and swims like mad for the tiny beach.

FELITI (SHOUTING)
What goes around comes around they say, so try not
to piss yourself SCUMBAG, as it only attracts them. I
heard you were a pretty good swimmer too!

FELITI watches without pity as the creature rips off CLIVE'S arm.
As FELITI remounts his bike he hears one last scream as CLIVE
goes under

#137 EXT.JABINGARRA FOREST.DAY

The last MEMBER of the DRUMLINE team is captured by WILL'S
LEAGUE MATES and they're really chuffed.

When all CAPTIVES are brought to the clearing the TV crew also
arrive and have a field day. They've got an award winning NEWS
story. JAPIE from DRUMLINE and two of the MINERS spill the
beans and the other KRANEK employees tell the rest.

KRANEK's done and some high level POLITICIANS and the
MAYOR and others are implicated and indicted.

#138 INT. WAYNTON PACIFIC OCEAN RIVER PUB. A MONTH
LATER

The whole town are celebrating having won a HIGH COURT
RULING and beaten all MINING LEASES IN RAINFOREST
VALLEY and RAINTREE.

The TOWNSPEOPLE now adjourn to the TOWN HALL to watch
the SENTINEL produced FILM cut of the LAST DAYS OF THE
BIG SKY. It's sombre viewing and is screened to enormous disgust,
but is also with pride and acclaim for the bravery of the CREW's
inspirational deaths.

WILL, JO, VICKY and WILL'S PARENTS all get an ovation at the
end of the screening.

#139 INT/EXT LONE PINE HOMESTEAD. DAY

VICKY, JOANNA, WILL AND LAUREN and his PARENTS are having a garden barbecue and they stand by NED'S grave and drink a toast to him.

> VICKY
> To the best of FATHERS I thought I'd never know but after his film was shown I know exactly what kind of person he was and I couldn't be prouder: Because of that FILM he will never totally be gone from life either. But, if I have lost my DAD, I have also gained a terrific UNCLE and GRANDPARENTS

She looks at LAUREN who's arm and arm with WILL And maybe even an AUNT...

Everyone laughs at this

> And I already have a wonderful MOTHER, so thank you DAD, thank you everything you have given me and for showing me what I have to do for the rest of my life. Rest in Peace DAD

EPILOGUE

> *SUPER: SEVERAL YEARS LATER*

#140 INT. KRANEK YACHT CORSAIR. DAY

KRANEK'S watching a replay of the TELEVISION SHOWS that have ruined him and he's drinking dangerously.

They're sailing smoothly for a while when there's a sudden massive crashing grating noise and the yacht starts to list. KRANEK and some crew members run to the viewing deck but the boat's already starting to sink.

FROM KRANEK'S VIEWING DECK POV THEY HAVE HIT SEVERAL HALF SUBMERGED CARGO SHIP CONTAINERS as lethal as icebergs to HIS YACHT.

THE CORSAIR starts to sink and KRANEK and the rest of the crew get into THE MOTORIZED LIFE BOAT AND HEAD FOR A NEARBY LOW LYING ISLAND WITH AN IMPOVERISHED GARBAGE-STREWN VILLAGE. HE gets off but the others go on without him. He PANICS WHEN HE SEES THE OLD ISLANDERS ARE INSTINCTIVELY PREPARING FOR DEATH AND THEY ARE ON THEIR KNEES AND TURNED TOWARDS A DISTANT SOUND WHICH IS UNMISTAKABLY A MASSIVE HUGE EXPLOSION. KRANEK'S Mobile rings and it's TORSTEN..

#141 SPLIT SCREEN:INT.HELICOPTER PT VILA & A DROWNING ISLAND

> TORSTEN ANDERSON
> Did you hear? It happened as VINCENT said it would. You've MUST get the CORSAIR to a sheltered PORT! Find high ground.

> KRANEK
> How high?

> TORSTEN (COLD, IRONIC)
> Are you anywhere near the HIMALAYAS? Even the SWISS ALPS would work.

> KRANEK
> You fucking DISLOYAL DANISH PRICK! I'm alone except for these scabrous ISLANDERS. And the CORSAIR is sinking before my eyes as we speak. What am I to do?

TORSTEN
The only thing you CAN do now AUGUSTIN: Make peace with your GOD and beg HIS forgiveness. And I don't mean the GOD MAMMON, I mean the God Currently known as JESUS CHRIST, JARWEH or ALLAH! May that GOD be with you at this time. And Pray for those innocent "scabrous" ISLANDERS because you helped make their lives the mess they've become. Good bye LITTLE KRAKEN!

The OLD ISLANDERS lie flat face down among the rubbish as the sun sets for the last time for them and they face what they know is coming. They kneel again and sing a POLYNESIAN song of lamentation and hold hands as the nightmare wave approaches and KRANEK joins them and holds hand in a final first and last bonding with ordinary people. They hear the wave like a roaring great jet liner approaching at ground level and just as fast. KRANEK'S face is like he sees GOD for the first time and he closes his eyes as the wave swallows them

FROM A CELESTIAL SATELLITE'S POV AS IN THE OPENING, BUT THIS WAVE IS MASSIVE AND SWALLOWS everything in its path. FADE TO BLACK

THE END

www.ingramcontent.com/pod-product-compliance
Lightning Source LLC
Chambersburg PA
CBHW030411120726
47904CB00007B/2235